Friends with (Social Security) Benefits

by
Elizabeth Barstone

Published by Haven Street Publishing

Contents

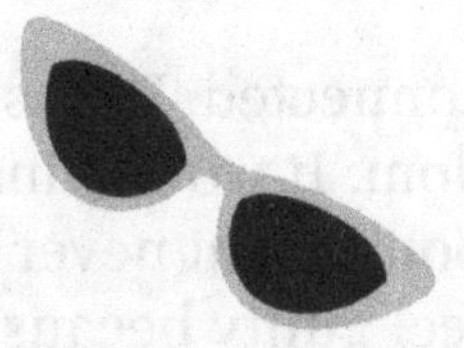

Chapter 1: The Check

"Ms. Philadelphia Powers!" The tall beefy Hollywood-style mailman proudly placed the envelope into my hands—the envelope I'd been counting down the minutes to receive.

"Thank you kindly, Richard!" I said. The mailman and I were on a first-name basis since I was always waiting for him in the lobby each morning—a habit I'd developed as soon as the post office had replaced our old mailman.

In rare form, I skipped the idle chitchat and hurried back up to my apartment, anxious to open my first taste of freedom. After forty years of working hard for multitudes of toxic corporations, the time had finally come—official retirement day!

Oh, I'd quit my last toxic corporate job months ago, but my frugal habits and sharp financial sense, not to mention an addiction to spreadsheets, had enabled me to live off my savings up to this point. I'd strategically budgeted my savings to get me through to this day. The third of July, exactly thirty days after turning 62.

The fear of getting old had been surpassed by the heady thrill of freedom, waiting just inside the envelope I clutched in my hands. According to my calculations, with my decade of tenancy at a rent-controlled building, combined with my frugal habits, it would be just enough to scrape by if I managed it right. I had three-and-a-half more weeks of enjoying cable TV before it would be disconnected. It was one of my willing cuts to ensure my freedom. It would finally give me time to read all the books I'd bought but never got around to reading. Reading made me feel guilty because my paid-for cable subscription just sat there, wasted, paid for and idle while I consumed another form of entertainment. Books kind of made me feel like I was cheating on cable TV.

I slammed the apartment door and ripped open the envelope.

It was at that point that I finally understood how people in car accidents say time suddenly goes in slow motion.

"Thirteen hundred dollars?" I shrieked. "How can it be thirteen hundred dollars?"

I yanked open the top drawer of my desk, now more a trophy to the last job I'd quit than anything else. It held my oversized artificial flowers—which beautified the entry just as well as real ones—and the drawers were still full of notebooks and pens. I pulled out my financial notebook and checked my plans.

According to my calculations, and according to a coworker who had just retired six months before I had, I should've been getting way more than *this!*

After forty-five minutes on hold and then a three-and-a-half-minute discussion with the powers that be, I was swiftly informed that my social security benefits would've been much higher if I'd been at the last corporation for more than three years.

"Well, that sucks!" I said to my useless phone after the call ended.

My mind instantly went into panic mode. Not the kind of panic mode that I assume most normal people get, but the kind where I begin mystery-solving and solution building. This overthinking skill was how I'd managed to get so many jobs so easily. Being the *only* problem solver in most of those companies was usually how I'd managed to quit so many jobs so readily. Not being afraid of change was how I'd managed to kick my cheating husband to the curb when I'd found out he'd had multiple affairs, one even during my pregnancy with my daughter, Jetta.

Now, here I was. A senior citizen with a monthly rent of $2000 and a monthly stipend of $1300.

My phone rang, and I was disappointed to see that it wasn't the government calling me back to tell me they'd made an egregious error and somehow had confused me with a hippie that had shunned work in favor of freedom. A lifestyle I'd been offered by a crazy boyfriend in my twenties—and now regretted not accepting. Perhaps I could've avoided a cheating husband, an unaffordable apartment, and the last forty years of stress due to corporate insanity. At least I'd have a secure camper van in the woods now. The phone rang for a third time in my hand while I wondered what Sunbow was up to now. He'd legally changed his name because he considered himself an optimistic rainbow of a guy. Anyway, I answered my daughter's call with a sigh.

"Hey, Jetta, what's up?" I asked, masking my anxiety over my newly discovered financial mess.

"Hey, Mom, David and I were talking and thought you might want to come stay the weekend," she said. "I know you hate parades, but we thought it would be fun, and you might like the fireworks."

"Okay, first of all, I don't *hate* parades," I pointed out. "I hated the idea of standing in the freezing cold to watch a Christmas parade last December when I could've watched it from my own living room window! But yes, I'll come."

Anything to get out of the house and give my mind

a break so that I could sort out what to do.

"Great, we can come pick you up," she suggested. "You can stay the night and then come with us on our picnic in the park tomorrow."

"No, I can drive," I said. I hated the way Jetta always tried to take control of everything.

"But Mom, traffic is crazy," she said. "Let us pick you up. Besides, it will help save on gas."

"No, I was just about to go out anyway, so I'll just pack a bag and be there in a half hour," I said. "Besides, it will save *you* two hours of having to charge up your electric car."

"But Mom—,"

"Bye, love you," I said and hung up.

If she'd been concerned about *me* saving on gas, that would've been thoughtful. But I was fed up with her constantly nagging me about how *I* was apparently single-handedly destroying the planet by driving my car, while she and her husband were frequently taking commercial jets for either business trips or vacations—and I highly doubted she'd discovered an electric-powered commercial jet!

The drive across the city gave me time to work out a way to explain my money situation. Jetta always inquired about my financial standing, as if she thought I was some braindead lunatic who didn't know how to manage a dollar. I, who had single-handedly raised her for most of her life and made sure she'd never gone without.

I was not wrong. I was inside their lovely little townhouse less than five minutes when she asked, "How are you doing for money, Mom?"

I was inclined to take the band-aid approach. "Well, I just got my first social security check."

"Oh, that's great," she said with a forced smile. "If

you need any help budgeting, David will help."

"Thanks, honey," I said as I heard the pitter pat-ter of grandchildren coming down the stairs in a hurried but orderly fashion. "But I'm sure I don't need a corporate CEO to help me sort out $1300."

"Thirteen Hundred Dollars!" Jetta stared at me like I'd asked her to watch me while I jumped off a cliff or something.

I waited.

"Thirteen hundred dollars? Mom, you can't survive on that! Your rent *alone* is *two thousand!*"

I nodded.

"Why don't you move in with us?" she asked imme-diately, without even taking a moment to think she might want to discuss that with her husband. Although, for all I knew, they may have *already* discussed it. I remembered how, when I was her age, how old I'd thought people in their sixties were. "We have a spare room. You'll get to spend more time with the grandkids!"

Speaking of which, Emily and Nathan walked po-litely into the room. "Grandmother!" they said in unison like well-behaved little robots.

I scooped them both up into big hugs, something they looked like they could use. "How are my little dar-lings?"

"We're fine, Grandmother," Nathan said far too maturely for a seven-year-old.

"Call me Grammy!" I said. I'd told them this hun-dreds of times, but they always began with the same re-served address. "No need to be so *formal;* we're family!" No matter how relaxed they became during our visits, it seemed as though their dull left-brained father and their wannabe-perfect mother had somehow brainwashed all sense of emotion from them by the time I visited again.

"Did you bring us anything?" Emily whispered in my ear.

"Emily!" Jetta scolded. "You know that is not polite! You are never to ask anyone that."

"I'm sorry," Emily said. "Please forgive me."

I raised my eyebrows at Jetta. While politeness was appealing, I feared she'd overdone it.

"Let me check and see if you guys are robots," I said, eyeing the kids up and down. "Have you ever injured a human being, or through inaction caused a human being to come to harm?"

They both shook their heads no and giggled at the familiar routine.

"Do you obey orders given you by a human being except where those orders might conflict with the first rule?" I asked with a mock serious expression.

Emily twisted up her mouth and looked at her mother. "Maybe," she said.

"Yes," Nathan said. "We obey orders."

"Hmm," I said. "Do you protect your own existence as long as it does not conflict with the first two Asimov laws of robotics?"

"I think," Nathan said.

"I don't know what that means," Emily said and looked at her mother. Jetta just stood there, arms folded, rolling her eyes impatiently as she waited to be the center of attention again.

"Well, you just *may* be robots," I said thoughtfully. I folded my arms and stared at the ceiling as if I were really trying to determine if my grandchildren were robots. They loved this; my daughter did not!

"Oh no!" Emily said. "Do the *final* test!"

"Okay, if you're sure," I said.

"Yes!" Nathan agreed.

"Jetta, do you have any pictures of traffic lights?" I asked, teasing an annoyed smile from her stern face. "No? Well, I guess I'll just have to do the last-resort test, but if you guys laugh, you are definitely *not* robots!" I reached out and tickled them. They both giggled and seemed to turn into natural children before my very eyes. "Ah well, I guess you're not robots after all."

Then I handed them each a chocolate bar. "Here, I picked these up for you guys at the gas station!"

"Mom!" Jetta said as the kids took the bars and seemed to come to life. "You know I limit the amount of sugar the kids have."

"It's a special occasion," I said. "Or are you annoyed because I went to the gas station? And besides, the sugary cereals you give the kids have ten times the amount of sugar as those chocolate bars!" I wasn't entirely sure that was accurate, but I knew neither one of us was going to check that out. The kids waited for her resigned nod before scampering into the kitchen, which was the only area they were allowed to have food.

I justified the occasional treats for the kids by the fact that I hardly ever saw them. Even though they just lived on the other side of the city, they had busier schedules than I had in my corporate jobs! Between piano lessons, tutoring, gymnastics, ballet, and speech therapy to make sure Emily didn't lisp, I normally had to book an appointment three weeks in advance just to see my grandkids!

"So, Mom," Jetta said now that the kids were out of earshot. "Seriously, you can't live on that little bit of money. What are you going to do? I think it might be good for all of us if you move in here."

I knew she didn't mean that last part—about it being good for *all* of us—but her look of concern seemed genuine. I hated the way she worried about me; she had enough on her plate. At the same time, I realized that even if I did go back to work, I couldn't work forever, and at some point, I would be facing this same crisis. And I was tired. Tired of corporations. Tired of giving away the hours of my life to employers and being too tired at the end of the day to enjoy any remaining hours that were supposedly mine. I wasn't getting any younger, and I was tired. Just tired.

Chapter 2: Frankie

The picnic was picture-perfect. I could expect no less from Jetta. She was the epitome of a perfect housewife—from the 1950s. I was proud of her. Sure, she was strict when it came to the kids, but at least the kids had manners. I'd seen enough public meltdowns from kids—and the red faces of their parents—to appreciate Jetta's parenting. She wasn't exactly a *fun* parent, but I could not fault her for choosing to be a firm *parent* instead of the *best friend* I'd been to her when she was a child.

"So, any decision yet?" she asked as David taught the kids how to fly kites some distance away.

"Jetta, moving from my home is a big decision," I reminded her. "I'd be moving from a large two-bedroom apartment into a tiny spare bedroom. Where am I going to put my furniture?"

"Well, you wouldn't *need* furniture," she said. "We have furniture. What more would you need?"

"Well, a place for my stuff," I said. "What about my desk?"

"You don't really *need* a desk, do you?" she said.

"I've used it for working in the evenings for the past forty years," I said. "I'm not going to get rid of it now." I didn't bother explaining that keeping that desk—even though I had no intention of returning to the corporate workforce—reminded me that I still *could* if I wanted to.

"Mom, you can't live in the past forever!" Jetta's exasperation was clear, her blue vein pulsing in her forehead.

"It's more like I'm living for the future," I replied. But just the mention of the past sent my mind drifting back to Sunbow with his solar oven and off-the-grid RV—those fleeting days of carefree bliss. Jetta's voice droned on while I escaped into the bright sunny days of the past, running through the woods with my first love—escaping a herd of bees after he'd decided to live off the land and raid a beehive for its honey. I was snapped back to the present by Jetta's sudden silence.

"Don't you think?" she asked, her eyebrows shooting up so high, they almost disappeared into her hairline—and she didn't even have bangs!

"About what?" I asked, not wanting to admit I'd been lost in my carefree days of my youth. Before marriage. Before work. And before Jetta.

"I don't want you to be struggling for money," she said. Her voice had turned into a high-pitched whine, fueled with worry.

"Honey, don't worry about me," I told her. "My rent is paid up until the end of the month, so I'm sure I will find a solution before then."

"Mom, that's three weeks away!" she said.

"Look, honey," I began, ready to educate her on my problem-solving skills, when David and the kids returned, and I was forced to curb my response. "Don't worry."

We waited until David had exchanged the kites for frisbees and then resumed.

"I need time to think about it," I said calmly. "It's a big move."

"Okay," she said. "But—uh oh!"

I whipped my head around to follow her gaze and my jaw dropped as well. Jetta was already on her feet running towards the elderly lady that was lying on the ground after being hit by David's frisbee. I scrambled to my feet and was right behind her.

I had visions of David being sued by the lady's family. Before we reached her, she was sitting up as David and the kids apologized profusely. *What a shame! A poor little old lady just out enjoying a picnic and then whack, hit by a wayward frisbee!*

"Are you okay, ma'am?" David fell to his knees beside her.

"I think so," the woman said, rubbing her head.

"Oh my goodness!" Jetta screamed as she joined David. "Are you alright?"

"I'm so sorry!" David repeated.

"Are you okay?" I asked, and as the woman looked up at me, a familiar face morphed into a shocked expression.

"Del?" she asked. "Del, is that you?"

It took me a second for my brain to rewind about forty years; to the last time I'd seen my best friend, Frankie. "Hootin' banana crackers! Frankie?" I could not believe it. This *old lady* was my best friend from high school and roommate for two years after we graduated. "I haven't seen you in, what, forty years?"

"I know, right?" Her look of awe and indignity at being hit by the frisbee morphed into shock and happiness. "I've missed you so much!"

I managed to push David out of the way and wrap my arms around my oldest best friend in the world. "How have you been? And how are you? And how is your head?"

"I'm fine," she said, rubbing her head. I examined it closely and there was no bump or bruise. That was Frankie; tough as nails.

"What are you doing in the city?" I gushed out. I'd left the small town of Rangeville and never looked back.

Not even when Frankie had moved back to marry Edgar and begged me to move back too so we could raise our families together. "How's the family?"

"If you're sure you're okay," David said, wanting approval before leaving us alone.

"I'm fine, I'm fine," Frankie insisted. "This must be your children."

"This is Jetta, my daughter," I said. "And this is David, her husband, and their two children, Nathan and Emily."

"Oh, what a beautiful family!" she said.

"Come join us," I suggested.

"Yes, please, come join us," David urged.

"Oh, I'm just waiting for my son to come back," she said. "I'm in the city for the weekend visiting my son, he'll be here any minute with his kids. I chose to wait here because I can't stand his ex."

"Understandable," I said—even though I didn't know her son, much less his ex! "I can sit with you until he gets back."

"Yes!" she said. With that, Jetta, David and the kids went back to their picnic blanket.

"Didn't you have two sons?" I asked Frankie.

"Yes, and two daughters," she said. "And they all live elsewhere except for Tommy who lives here in the city."

"Oh, I'm so happy to see you again!" I repeated. "So, tell me about what's happening with you!"

"Well, Edgar is no longer with us as of two years ago," she said, and instantly her smile faded into a grim shadow. "I had to sell the house and move into a tiny apartment."

"Oh no, I'm so sorry to hear that!" I said. "Wow, you guys were married a long time!"

"It would've been forty years this September," she

said mournfully. "He was a good man. I just don't know what I'm going to do without him."

"I know it must be hard," I said. I wanted to encourage her by telling her she already *was* doing without him, for an entire two years apparently. But she didn't look like she was ready for that kind of eye-opener.

"You should move to the city!" I urged. "It would be like old times!"

"I can't afford that," she said with an air of resignation. "Edgar was always giving me surprises, and he didn't fail to surprise me even after he moved. Turns out he was so far in debt that his entire life insurance was gone immediately. Then there was a bureaucratic glitch that prevented me from getting spousal benefits, so I have nothing."

"Moved?" I asked. "You said he *died.*"

"Oh, don't say the D word!" she said, looking mortified. "I prefer to say Edgar has moved to Heaven. It makes it easier. That way it's like he's still living, just somewhere else."

"Oh," I said. "Well, I do believe in an afterlife. So, he *is* still living somewhere."

"That's what I think too," she said.

"So, come live with me!" I suggested, suddenly realizing that I sounded just like Jetta. The offer was out of my mouth before I had a chance to think. "I've got lots of space! I have a two-bedroom right here in the city. It will be like old times again! It will be fun!"

"Oh gosh, remember how we would stay up half the night talking about the guys downstairs?" She asked and her old familiar smile tugged at her face. It seemed like old memories gave her the strength to push aside her pain, even for just a moment.

"Oh, I know!" I remembered. "I had the hots for Michael—and what was the name of that other guy?"

"Jerry!" she said, and her eyes twinkled like old times. "Oh, he was so gorgeous."

"And remember when they invited us down for dinner?" I reminded her.

"Oh, I thought we invited them for dinner," she said.

"Well, we tried," I reminded her with a laugh. "And then they felt bad about turning us down, and that's why they invited us down the following week. Remember?"

"Oh yes," she said and laughed. "And we found out *why* they had no interest in us."

"Well, how were *we* to know that *they* were a couple?" I said. "At least they turned out to be great friends and neighbors."

"Oh, we had so much fun back then!" she said with an air of longing. "I wish we could just turn back the hands of time and live in those days again."

"We can!" I insisted. "Come live with me! It'll be fun! It'll be just like old times!"

"I'll think about it," she said. "The thought of moving again is not as appealing as the root canal the dentist insists that I get."

"I know," I said. "Trust me, I know."

"Oh, here comes Tommy," she said. "And my grandkids!"

I waited and went through the introductions before politely excusing myself and leaving them to their family picnic, but not before exchanging phone numbers with Frankie. "Think about it," I said as I walked away. The truth was, I *needed* her to say yes, as much as I *wanted* her to. And I *really* hoped she would!

Chapter 3: The Cereal Fiasco

The fireworks weren't the only show that evening. I got to watch Jetta prove her superior parenting powers to nearby families by outfitting the kids with noise-cancelling headphones to shield their ears. It stopped being funny when she tried to wrangle a pair onto *me*. Then she and David dutifully donned their own after I declined. "You should protect your ears!" Jetta insisted, ironically shouting because she couldn't hear herself—and totally oblivious about the school dances I'd attended in my youth, where I'd planted myself as close to the speakers as possible.

In the morning, David left early for work despite it being Saturday, and Jetta slept late. Apparently being out so late the night before had left her exhausted—and by late, I mean eleven o'clock—so I got up with the kids.

"How about bacon and eggs for breakfast?" I asked, eyeing the neat row of sugary cereals on top of the fridge.

"We have cereal," Emily said.

"I *see that*," I said. "Why don't we just switch things up today?"

"Mom's really strict about breakfast," Nathan said, climbing down from the stool at the counter and pointing at the meal schedule taped to the fridge. Both kids looked uncomfortable as they watched me, probably wondering if I dared to defy their mom's regimented cereal rules. Jetta had laid out every meal for every day, along with every drink.

"Man, my last office wasn't this organized," I said, opening the fridge. "Well, unfortunately, today we will have to break that routine."

"We can't," Nathan said.

"Why not?" I asked, reaching for the eggs.

"Mommy says routines keep us from chaos," Emily said.

"Do you even know what chaos means?" I asked her. Her surprised face told me no.

"Okay, fine," I said and watched the tension melt from their little faces as soon as I returned the eggs to the fridge. I plopped down two cereal bowls in front of them and reached for the nearest box.

When I turned around with the box, their wide eyes told me all I needed to know. Nathan pointed to the correct box for Saturday.

"Well, your perfectly organized mother forgot to buy milk," I said to the kids. They looked as though I'd just told them the world was coming to an end. "Don't worry, I'm a problem solver."

The two watched in awe as I pulled a tub of chocolate ice cream down from the freezer and plopped two scoops on the top of each bowl of cereal. "Don't worry, it will melt into milk." They exchanged worried glances before shrugging and digging in.

The old-fashioned yellow phone attached to the kitchen wall suddenly rang and scared me out of my wits. The kids giggled. "I didn't know that works!" I'd thought it was just an ornament, but no, a working retro wall phone screamed of Jetta, considering she was apparently going for the perfect 1950s housewife and family.

"Answer it," Emily said.

"Yes, ma'am!" I said with a smile and picked up the receiver. "Hello?"

"Hello, am I speaking with a . . . Mrs. Philadelphia Powers?" a man asked.

"Yes," I said slowly and waited, feeling like I'd stepped back into the eighties as I held the receiver to my ear. "Can I help you with something?"

"It's Dunn Final Arrangements, and I'm calling about your headstone," he said.

"My what?" I shouted in his ear. Was this some kind of joke? *And why would anyone be calling me here—at Jetta's house?*

"The headstone you purchased last week," he said. "I just need to verify the spelling and to get your correct date of birth for it."

"Excuse me, . . .*what?*" I asked again, unable to wrap my head around the fact that there was a man wanting to get my name spelled correctly on a headstone—and calling *me* at my daughter's house!

"Your headstone," he said, irritated. "It came half off with the grave plot."

"Okay, somehow I think you have the wrong number?" I said, even though he had my name correct. "It's probably a computer glitch or something."

"Is this Philadelphia Powers?" he asked.

"Yes," I said, still confused.

"Okay, well, just a second," he said. So, I waited just a second. "Oh wait, okay. Okay the name on the receipt is Jetta Finch. Is *she* there?"

"That's my daughter," I said. "Is this a joke?"

"No ma'am," the guy said. "Your daughter purchased the last remaining plot in row 45B in Section C."

"Okay, and it's for *me?*" I asked in surprise.

"That's right," he said. "We just couldn't figure out if Philadelphia was your *name* or your birthplace."

"Okay, well of all people, *you* should know that it's

bad luck to put a name on a headstone of a living person," I said, trying to remember if that was actually true or not. "And second of all, you're saying my daughter is getting my *grave* ready?"

"Well, it's more like preparations so that no one has to deal with it during a time of crisis," he said.

"So, what, you just came around door to door and talked her into buying this?"

"No, no," he said quickly. "Not at all. She came down to our office and picked it out herself. We do not sell final arrangements door to door, ma'am. That would be . . . tactless."

"She will have to call you back," I said and hung up.

It was then that Jetta came down the stairs.

"Who was that?" she asked, coming into the kitchen. "What are you guys *eating!*"

"Ice cream cereal," Emily said. She had chocolate all over her chin. "It was dee-lish!"

Nathan slowly pushed his bowl away from him. It was empty and the only evidence of chocolate ice cream was the brown film on the inside of the bowl.

"Why are *my* children eating ice cream?" Jetta demanded. "For *breakfast!*"

"Because *someone* forgot to buy milk," I said pointedly. "And your children are so scared to stray from your rigid schedules that this was as close as we could get to your mandatory requirements. Heaven forbid they eat something *totally* off the charts like bacon and eggs!"

She looked offended.

"But since we're asking questions," I continued. "Why don't *you* tell *me* why you've already purchased my grave and headstone, complete with my name on it!"

She opened her mouth but didn't say a word for a minute. "How did you . . .um?"

"That's who was on the phone," I said. "Some guy wanting to get my name right on my headstone."

"Can we talk about this later?" she asked pointedly. "Let's get your face washed up, Emily!" Jetta pulled open a kitchen drawer—that in any *normal* home would've been a junk drawer—and pulled out a neat white facecloth from a neatly arranged row. She wet it under the tap and washed Emily's face. "Why don't you two go get dressed and then you can watch cartoons for an hour, okay?"

I was tempted to just storm out and get in my car, but my bag was upstairs, and I was apparently frozen in place by shock. When the kids were out of the room, she turned to me.

"I'm sorry, Mom," she said. "I didn't plan on you finding out like this."

"Right, because it would never come up until I'm gone, right?" I said. "Just because I turned 62, it doesn't mean I'm ready for the grave!"

"Mom, stop, it's not like that and you know it," she said, grabbing bread out of the fridge.

"Then tell me what it *is* like," I said. "You're constantly reminding me that I'm over the hill and can't take care of myself."

"For heaven's sake, Mom!" she said, sounding like the teenager she used to be.

"I'm not gonna move in with you, Jetta," I said. "Just like I couldn't follow insane rules and routines in toxic corporations, I cannot live in a house where your child is afraid that he might eat the wrong box of cereal because it hasn't been assigned for that day!"

"Mom!" she screamed as I turned to walk up the stairs to get my stuff. *"You can't even afford your rent!"*

"Then I will move to a smaller apartment," I said as she followed me up the stairs. "Or I can take in a roommate. The possibilities are endless when you think outside the box, Jetta!"

I grabbed my bag and hurried down the stairs, proving to us both just how much life I had in me! "I have a lot of living to do yet!" I said as I stormed out the door.

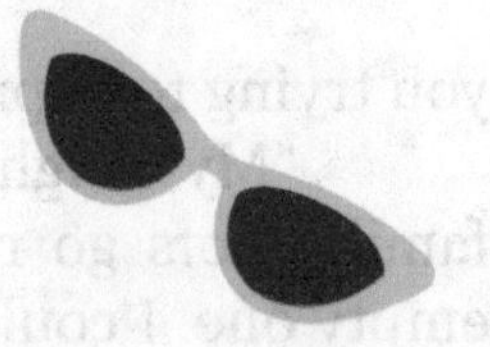

Chapter 4: Between Frankie, Del, and the Mailman

Even though I'd only been gone two nights, crawling into my own bed on Saturday night made me realize I'd never be able to sleep in Jetta's uncomfortable spare bed—even if she hadn't bought me a grave. Before I went to sleep, I sent her a text and told her I loved her. I knew Jetta; her heart was in the right place, somehow. But that didn't mean that I was ready to let her plan out the rest of my life. I was only 62 for heaven's sake. I was in pretty good health, so I might live another 30 years or more, and with medical science these days, I might even make it to 120! *Well, that was my plan.*

Despite the late hour, she texted me back a heart emoji and called me the next morning.

"Mom, look, I'm sorry," she said immediately. "Please just let me explain."

"You don't have to, honey," I said. "I know you just like to keep things in order and plan ahead. I understand. But I would appreciate it if you don't plan *that* far ahead for *me*, okay?"

"Well, to be honest, I *didn't* really," she said.

"Didn't really what?"

"The grave," she said. "I mean, I wasn't really *trying* to buy your grave. I only *needed* to buy it so that the Rosses didn't get it."

"What? Who are the Rosses?" I asked. "And why are

you trying to deprive them of a grave?”

“My neighbor, Gloria Ross,” she explained. “Her family plots go right up to Daddy’s except for that last empty one. I couldn’t let her have it because I figured *you* should be the one buried next to Daddy.”

“Oh, honey, it doesn’t matter to *me* where I’m buried,” I assured her. “It’s not like I’m going to be *living* there! I expect I’ll be moving to heaven.” *Hmm. Frankie was right. That is a way better way to phrase it!*

“Well, still, I thought *you* should be the one buried next to Daddy,” she said.

“Aw, honey,” I said. “I know you were just a kid when we got divorced, so I never wanted to badmouth your father. But the truth is, we didn’t get along all that great. I honestly don’t care if I’m never buried next to someone I wasn’t happy with. And besides, I just don’t think those kinds of details matter all that much.”

“Well, they matter to *me*, Mom,” she said. I could tell she was quietly crying.

“It’s okay, honey,” I said. “Whatever you want. It’s already bought and paid for, so let’s just forget it, okay?”

“Well, I bought it with the money that Daddy left me,” she said. “I hadn’t touched it because I was so mad at him. But I just thought it would be better if you two were buried next to each other because you guys were once married . . . and you don’t have anyone else.”

“Oh, Jetta,” I said. “Don’t worry about me. If that’s what *you* want, fine; bury me next to your father. Just don’t count on it happening anytime soon.”

“You know I worry about you,” she said. “You don’t really have much of a life.”

“I am doing fine!” I said. “Remember, I’m a problem solver! I will fix this! When have I ever *not* fixed things?”

“I know,” she said. “But seriously, if you can’t find

a solution in the next three weeks, then will you move in with me?"

"Only if I can bring my own bed," I said.

Our conversation moved into more mundane things, and I asked her about her working retro phone.

"Well, when we got the house, we tried to remove it, but we found a hole behind it, and David didn't know how to fix holes, so we just put the phone back and figured we may as well get it activated."

We chuckled for a moment, and I was happy we'd finally found something funny we could smile about.

"Mom, I wanted to tell you something while you were here, but I didn't get a chance," she said.

"Okay, I can't see how there could be any bigger surprise than there being a grave with my name on it, but go ahead," I said, determined to keep the whole grave thing as light as possible.

"Well, how would you feel about having another grandchild?" she asked casually.

"What? Are you serious?" I almost spilled my coffee.

"We're having another baby!" Her voice was high pitched and filled with excitement.

"Oh, that is so wonderful!" I said, suddenly feeling bad for our conflict earlier. "I'm so happy for you! That is, if *you're* happy."

"Of course we're happy!" she said.

"I'm so happy for you, honey!" I said.

I was glad that we'd managed to work everything out back to the status quo in our relationship, something that we always seemed to do before and after a visit, but never *during.*

With an eased mind, I slept Sunday night, and in the morning, I couldn't be sure which woke me up first, the sun glaring in my window assuring me that a beautiful day was on its way, or the ringing phone. *It was Frankie!*

"Hey!" I said, pretending like I'd been awake for ages, even though it was only nine in the morning, the first Monday morning of my *official* retirement.

"I was thinking I could drop by and visit before heading back home this afternoon," she said. "If it's okay with you."

"Of course!" I said, throwing the blankets off me and getting up. My place was sort of a mess and that wouldn't do for company. When we hung up, I made coffee and cleaned the entire apartment like I was bionic. I barely had enough time to get out of the shower and dress before Frankie buzzed my apartment.

"Come on up!" I yelled into the intercom and pressed the button to unlock the lobby door. I took a glance around the apartment. It had been transformed from a place that looked *very* lived in to a place I would *want* to live in. I promised my future self I would keep it this way.

When she walked through the door, it took a moment for me to see my old friend—that I'd seen just yesterday—standing there in a foreign, older body. I'd been so excited to see her the day before that I'd blocked out how old she'd looked to me at first. But when she spoke, it was *her*. My best friend. And it was like no time had passed. She was still the same. And so was I.

We chatted over coffee, and I showed her the apartment.

"So, do you think you will move in, and we can be roomies like when we were young?" I asked with high hopes.

"Well, like I said, a move is a huge deal," she said. "And I'm broke, so I can't really afford the extra expense of a moving truck."

"Can't Tommy help you?" I asked.

"Well, I hate to impose on him," she said.

"He's your son," I said. "Of course he would help you. Plus, he might like having you closer. You know how our kids like to keep an eye on us."

"You're right about that," she said. "But I don't know." Just like she always had been, Frankie wasn't one to make snap decisions. Every major decision required a lot of thought and a long list of pros and cons. I showed her my second bedroom which was a library/sewing room/arts and crafts room.

"Oh, I love it!" she said. "I like doing crafts too!"

"Well, I'll move my stuff out if you want the bedroom," I said. "I'll put them all in my room."

"Or, and I'm not promising anything by saying this," she said. "But what if we shared a room like we did back in that tiny apartment in our twenties, and then this room could be a craft room for both of us!"

"Sure," I said. "But honestly, I really don't mind moving all my stuff into the living room so you can have your own room."

"But what about all *my* craft stuff and books?" she asked. "If I keep all my stuff in one room, I'd end up just being stuck in my room all day. Besides, I miss the days when we used to be roomies and stay up half the night eating chips and gossiping."

We laughed and it was instantly like old times.

"Well, sure, but remember back then, if one of us brought a boyfriend home, the other one had to sleep on the couch?"

"I don't know about you," she said. "But I won't be bringing any guys home."

"So, you'll do it? You'll move in?" I asked. "We can split the rent, and we won't have to worry about expenses so much."

"I don't know, Del," she said in her wishy-washy way that always drove me nuts. "I really need to think about it. But I'll let you know."

"Okay," I said, working extra hard not to be pushy.

When Tommy texted that he was back to pick her up, I walked Frankie down to the lobby just as the mailman arrived.

"Oh Richard!" I said, acting like we were on better terms than we actually were. "I'd like you to meet my best friend of all time, Frankie. Frankie, this is our mailman, Richard."

"Hello, Frankie," Richard said with his usual wide grin. "It's a pleasure to meet you. Are you moving into the building?"

"Why yes, I *am!*" she said enthusiastically, her face lighting up. I felt my heart soar—not just because my rent problem was solved, but because I could see my old friend turning back into her old self before my very eyes. *Thank you, Hollywood-style mailman!*

As I walked her out, she asked, "Why didn't you tell me you had a movie star delivering your mail?"

"Because I wanted you to love me for me," I said coyly, and we both burst out laughing. "So, you will? Really?"

"To be honest, I was already heavily leaning toward a yes," she confided. "But after getting a load of your mailman, that sealed it!" She seemed like her old self. Full of life and smiles. And so was I.

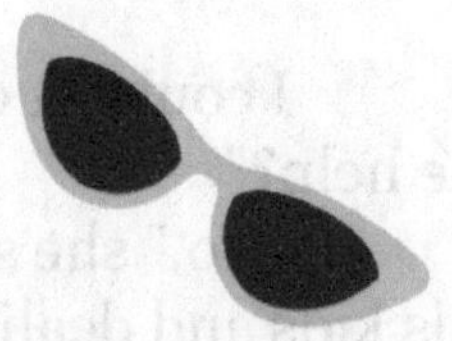

Chapter 5: A Shrine and a Truck

It took four days of calling before I finally managed to reach Frankie. I barely had three weeks to make August's rent payment and with no word from her, I was getting antsy.

"I've been trying to call you for days," I said when she finally picked up.

"I'm sorry, Del," she said. Her voice sounded tired like she'd just woken up. "I've been meaning to call you."

"Well, I figured you were busy packing and getting ready for the move," I said, making it clear what my level of expectation was.

"Yeah," she said slowly. "About that."

I waited and there was no rest of her sentence. *"And?"* I finally asked.

She sighed loudly into the phone. "I'm sorry, but I just won't be able to move," she said.

"What?" I shrieked. It was instinctive, not like I intended to yell into her ear.

"Yeah," she said. "I just can't."

Well, *that* wouldn't do! I deserved more of an explanation than that! "What do you mean?" I asked. "Why? What happened?"

"It's a big move, and I have no one to help me," she said. "I can't afford movers, and I can't drive a moving truck."

I couldn't either. "Well, what about Tommy? Won't he help?"

"No," she said. "He's too busy with work and seeing his kids and dealing with his ex."

"Yeah, but moving only takes one day!" I said. "What's wrong with him? You're his own mother, and he can't take *one* day to help his mother move?"

"He's really busy," she said. "And I would have to break my lease here. I just can't do it right now. Maybe next year."

"Don't worry," I said. "I'll find you a moving truck! Even if I have to drive it myself!"

"Don't worry about it," she said. She sounded old and tired. She didn't sound like the same person who had been in my apartment just days before and was enamored with my mailman. "Listen, I have some things I have to do, so I have to go, but I'll call you back later, okay?"

I had no choice but to let her hang up. But I was not going to give up! I looked up her son's number and gave him a call. He was at work and had to put me on hold while he found a private spot to talk.

"You're Mom's friend, right?" he asked, obviously trying to piece together why an old lady like me would be calling him out of the blue.

"Yes, and you're her son, right?" I said pointedly.

"Yes, I'm Mom's son," he said with a little chuckle. "What can I help you with?"

"It's not *me* that needs your help!" I said, waving my hand around as if he could see me. "It's your mother. Why can't you even take one day out of your busy little life to help your mother move? She had agreed to move in with me, and because you won't even help her, she's going to remain stuck in that tiny little town in a tiny little apartment all by herself! Do you think that's very fair? She doesn't have that many years left, you know, why not help her re-store some joy to her life?"

When I was finished my rant, there was silence on the other end, and I was about to ask if he was still there when he responded.

"Okay, I'm confused," he finally said. "Is *that* what she told you? That I didn't want to help her move?"

"Yes, I just got off the phone with her!" I said. I'd like to see him try to lie his way out of that!

"She told me about your offer, and I told her it's a *great idea,*" he said. "I'd feel better if she lived here in the city, and I told her I'd even help her move. She told me she can't bear to leave the town where Dad is buried. I couldn't talk her out of it. I even promised to drive her back to see Dad's grave whenever she wanted, but she didn't want to budge. I think it would be a *very* good idea for her to be near friends. She's got herself isolated in a tiny little apart-ment, and she isn't having any kind of a life at all."

So, she lied to me!

"So, to be clear," I said. "If I can convince her to move, you will get a truck and help?"

"Absolutely," he promised. "But I'll warn you, my mother isn't easily moved. If you can get her to budge, I'll be surprised."

"Oh, I'll get her to budge," I vowed. "I'm not going to let my oldest best friend waste away all alone. No way!" Not when this would solve *both* of our problems. It was clear that Frankie needed me as much as I needed her. She just didn't know it yet!

When Jetta called to see how I was doing and how my roommate agenda was coming along, I assured her everything was on track because they soon would be—be-cause I was in charge of my own track!

The following morning, I drove the four hours to

Rangeville. I had to stop at three different gas stations to use the bathroom, which is the main reason I never looked back after moving to Davenport. Besides being afraid of heights, I was phobic about public washrooms. I wasn't going to put myself at risk of getting germs unless there was absolutely no other choice. I just hoped Frankie could appreciate me risking my life to save her from a future of doom and loneliness.

With the help of GPS, directions from Tommy, and memorizing the building from a street view of the map, I easily found her building. It hadn't been there when I'd left Rangeville forty years ago. In fact, hardly anything was the same. Some of the same downtown buildings were there, but they were no longer Radio Shack, IGA and Blockbuster. Now they were dollar stores, tattoo parlors, and co-working spaces.

I'd wanted to surprise her, but I had to buzz her apartment for her to let me in.

"What are you doing here?" Frankie asked from her doorway as I made my way up a flight of six steps.

"I came to visit," I said. "Tommy failed to mention you didn't have an elevator."

"It's only a few steps," she said.

"Are you sick?" I asked as I stepped inside of her dark apartment. "Why are the lights off?" The only light was from a large TV set on the other side of the apartment by a window with drawn drapes. The small apartment was filled with boxes stacked everywhere, leaving only a path from the entry to the sofa in front of the television, and to the bathroom and bedroom. It was like a cardboard maze.

"I hardly need to put the lights on," she said as she flicked the light switch on. "And power is expensive."

"We can at least open the drapes and get some light in here," I said, picking my steps carefully to the window, worried that I'd trip and fall and break a hip just trying to open some drapes. *No wonder she didn't want to move. This was way too much stuff to even fit into my apartment!* "I see you've been packing."

"No, that's Edgar's stuff mostly," she said. "I never really unpacked when I moved in here."

With the drapes opened, the light of day shone on the sadness of her little hovel.

"I keep the drapes closed because the nosy man in that building next to us is always staring at me from his window," she explained, peering nervously over my shoulder to see if he was there.

"Oh," I said, glancing around. It was clear from the stacks of opened boxes with various items strewn and piled that she'd only dug through boxes to get items as she'd needed them. "How long have you been living here?"

"A year and three months and nine days," she said.

"Wow, that's a specific answer," I said. "So, tell me again why you prefer this place, where you can't even open your curtains, over living with me?"

"It's not that I *prefer* it," she said. "It's just that I *can't* move. I have no one to help me."

"I'll help you," I said. "And I talked to Tommy yesterday, and he said *he* will rent a truck and help."

"Oh, you spoke to Tommy?" she asked, and I knew that *she* knew that I knew what was going on.

"Yes, and he will move you," I said. "So, unless you have *another* reason why you want to live in *this,* that means you can move in with me!" I smiled. I waved my arms in optimistic enthusiasm, but her reaction caught me off guard. She burst into tears!

"What is wrong?" I asked, instinctively maneuvering over to her and enveloping her in my arms. "What did I say?"

"I just can't," she sobbed into my shoulder. "I can't leave here. This is where Edgar is. I can't leave him."

"Tommy said he'd drive you back here whenever you want to visit Edgar," I said. "And I will too!"

"No, here! He's here!" Frankie pulled away and waved her arms all around. "All this stuff is his. I can't part with it. It's *him*. It's all I have left of him!"

"It's okay," I said quickly, before I could even think *how* it would be okay. I just needed her to stop crying before I joined in. "You don't have to get rid of it. We can figure this out."

"But none of this stuff will fit in your apartment," she said. "It's not fair to make you move your stuff just so I can move all my stuff in."

I grasped her hands. "We'll figure this out," I assured her. "Together! Let's figure out what you can't part with. You don't need to keep everything, right? Just keep what Edgar would want you to have."

"I need it *all,*" she said. She looked hopeless. "I just don't know what to do! I just can't go on like this! I can't handle it!" She pulled her hands out of mine and covered her eyes, sitting down on a sole empty kitchen chair.

"Okay, look," I said, kneeling in front of her and grasping her arms gently. I remembered how Jetta had tried to make me get rid of my desk so that I could move in with her. "Listen, I'm here to help! I will help you go through the boxes and decide what to bring to my apartment. The rest, we can bring to Davenport with us and put it in a self-storage unit, okay? You can keep it *all!* And you'll be able to have access to it whenever you want. Or maybe Tommy will keep it in *his* garage, and you'll be able to see it whenever you want. Or, if you need to keep it even closer, I have a small storage unit in the parking garage of my building. I can clean that out and get rid of stuff I don't use anymore, and it's all yours! I *promise*. You can put *all* of Edgar's stuff in it, and then you can go down and go through it any time you like. Even in the middle of the night, if you want! And you can keep some of it in the apartment."

"Really?" she asked, looking at me with red eyes that had obviously spent too much time crying in the past two years. "You'd seriously give up your storage area for me?"

"If you're living with me, it will be *our* storage area," I pointed out. "And you need it more than I do."

"Do you really think it would work?" she asked, hesitantly, but I could see that she was beginning to see the faint light at the end of the tunnel.

"We will *make* it work," I said. "Things never just work out by themselves. We have to *make* it work out. We can do this! And it will be just like old times!"

"It's going to take a lot of work to move," she said, looking around as if she was suddenly realizing the physical weight of her emotional baggage.

"When has work ever hurt us?" I asked.

"I *guess* we could try it," Frankie said, and I could tell by the way she was willing to blink back the tears that it would be just like old times indeed!

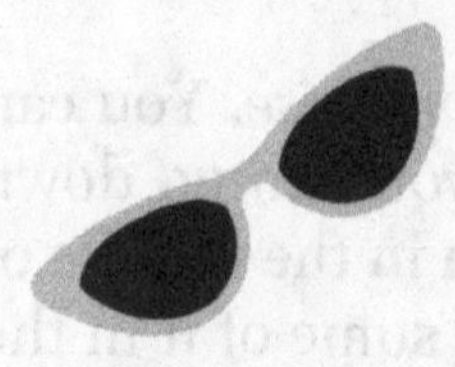

Chapter 6: Never Got To Do

Before the end of July, Frankie arrived with all her belongings, and Tommy helped carry all the boxes of his father's stuff to the storage room behind my parking spot. I had emptied it the day before by throwing away what I couldn't give away.

"Here is the key to the storage room," I said, taking the small key off my keychain and handing it to her. "It's all yours."

She took it and looked wistful as she stared into the small room with Edgar's boxes stacked to the ceiling. "It's so hard to just lock the door," she admitted. "It feels wrong to just lock him up all the way down here."

"Think of it this way," I said, reaching in and turning off the light in the room, trying to get her started. "Think of this as being Edgar's room. You can come visit him whenever you want. Okay?"

I wasn't sure if my words were helpful, but at least she was moving forward a step at a time, and that had to be a good thing.

She nodded and slowly closed the door and turned the key. She turned to face me with determination in her eyes, and I wasn't sure she would be able to take a step away from the door. Thankfully my car was right in front of us. "Let me take you out to dinner," I said. "To celebrate the first day of being roomies!"

She nodded silently and we went out for burgers and

fries. "Just like the olden days," she said, scarfing down a burger. "I haven't eaten fast food for about ten years because I've been on this diet."

"No offence," I said but stopped myself from informing her that her diet wasn't working. "But we're too old to deny ourselves the joys of life. And if today the joys of life include a burger and fries, then so be it!"

"So be it!" Frankie raised what was left of her burger to make a toast with mine.

"So be it!" I said again, and somehow, it was like our new motto.

When we got back to the building, I dropped her off at the front entrance. I said she could check the mail on her way in, and I'd meet her at the apartment after I parked the car. I had a feeling if she exited the car in the garage, I would end up having to surgically remove her from the storage room.

We spent the evening setting up her bed in my room and immediately, I felt like we were forty years younger. We talked until our sentences were consistently interrupted by yawns, and then somewhere between our memories, I was asleep. I woke up to go to the bathroom around four and on my way back to bed, I noticed that her bed was empty. Well, I knew for a fact that she wasn't in the bathroom, so I checked our craft room. Nope. Empty.

I knew where she was, but I decided it was better not to disturb her. Obviously, she would need some time to adapt. I knew I needed to let her have that time. *But was it healthy for her?* I had no idea. I decided at least for tonight, for the first night, I would let her be. I would let her cry in the garage if she needed to, but after tonight, I would push her out of her past, the way a mother bird pushes her babies out of the nest. She might cry, but she would fly! Even to *me,* that sounded harsh, but my best friend was in a rut—or worse, in a *hole,* because even a rut has some direction to allow movement.

Despite my resolve to not interfere, as the hours ticked by, and she still didn't return, I concocted visions of her sprawled out in the storage room sobbing uncontrollably, and it broke my heart. I knew I had to do something.

I got up and grabbed my housecoat. I wasn't going to bother getting dressed at six in the morning just to go to the storage room. The odds of running into anyone in my housecoat would be rare. But oh no, odds will be whatever they want to be, and I vigorously stepped into the elevator in my pink fluffy housecoat only to be greeted by the super who was on his way down to the lobby with a mop and bucket. I didn't let on that I thought my attire was anything but ordinary, and he had no choice but to go along with it, nod, and bid me a good day as he exited.

When I reached the storage room, sure enough, Frankie was in there, but she wasn't crying. Although from the way she was hugging the box of tissues, it was clear she had been. To my surprise none of the boxes were opened. I'd had visions of her being draped in all his clothes or something. But no, the boxes were still stacked neatly, and she was sitting neatly in her nightdress and housecoat, staring into space, obviously lost in thought. If she had been crying earlier, she'd drained herself of tears.

I tapped on the open door. "Good morning," I said. "Are you okay?"

She nodded and scrambled to her feet. "It's just," she said. "I just . . . I couldn't."

"I know," I said gently. "It's okay. Do you want to open the boxes and go through his stuff?"

She shook her head. "No, I haven't opened them since he moved," she said.

"Okay, well, why don't we open one now?" I suggested. She was in obvious need of different tactics. It was almost like she was hiding from his stuff, but somehow felt more comfortable having it hidden and all around her at the same time.

"I can't *bear* to see his clothes without him in them," she said. I didn't know what to say to that. I debated telling her that even when he was alive, he wasn't in *all* his clothes at the same time. But I couldn't really understand what she was going through, so I kept my mouth shut for fear of making it worse.

"I know, but what if we just, I don't know, take a peek to make sure they didn't get dusty from the moving truck?" I suggested, thinking that perhaps if she *did* something—anything at all—she would at least be moving forward. Perhaps even just looking at his stuff might make her somehow release whatever was holding her back. I just made the suggestion and let her make the decision.

"That might be a good idea," she agreed slowly, clearly considering the potential pros and cons. She reached for a smaller box and tore at the tape that had kept it shut for over two years. She opened it and pulled out a pair of his blue pajamas, neatly folded for so long that the creases looked like gray lines through the blue plaid pattern. She held them for a moment and gently set them down. She pulled out a few of his tee shirts and then set the empty box aside. "You know, Edgar only ever wore one pair of pajamas."

The fact that seeing his clothes got her talking instead of crying *had* to be a good sign, I concluded.

"Okay," I said, unsure of how to end this moment. "Let's go back upstairs and have some coffee. You still have a ton of boxes to unpack up there."

"I think I'll take these upstairs with me," she said, holding onto the pajamas while putting his shirts back into their box.

"Okay," I said. At least she was making progress. If she needed to have an item of her late husband's close to her, then so be it. I had never had to deal with what she was going through; I'd been divorced for twenty years when Fred had died. I hadn't lost a lifelong partner; I'd lost an ex—and I'd lost him *many* years before that.

I helped her unpack several boxes of her belongings and cleared shelf space for her. As she pulled things from each box, she relayed stories of where she bought them or when Edgar had given them to her. Her belongings showed me her life story better than any history book could have.

As box after box was emptied, I could see sparks of her old self shine through. Notebooks and lists filled up many of her boxes. I wasn't that surprised. That was something we'd always had in common. She pulled out a pile of papers that turned out to be a bunch of *to-do* lists. Very few items on the lists had been checked off.

"These are just garbage," she said, quickly crumpling the papers and heading to the kitchen garbage bin, but I'd already seen her embarrassment at her unaccomplished goals.

"Wait until you see *my* to-do lists!" I said. I went to my desk drawer and pulled out my notebook. I proudly opened it to show her page after page of *to-do* lists, with lots of things unchecked. Partially because I was a procrastinator, and partially because after I got busy tackling the lists, I forgot all about the list itself, and never went back to check things off. "See, that's why we've always been best friends. We're listers!"

She smiled broadly and went back to unpacking her box. She pulled out another handful. "Oh, here's more. Oh, this is from a few years ago. I'd made a list of things I wanted to do in 2015. I clearly didn't check off *take a cruise*."

"Oh, I think I had that on one of my 2012 lists," I said, and we laughed.

"I still haven't done stuff on my Y2K list!" she said.

"Well, not to brag, but I still haven't done things from my list I made in the 1980s," I said, and we laughed even more. "Remember I always had *be in a movie* on almost every single list?"

"Oh, I remember our teenage lists! On every single one, at the very top of the list, we had plans to go to Hollywood and wrangle a date with Brake Caldwell!" Frankie laughed as though no time had passed since then.

"Ah, yes, Brake Caldwell," I said with an air of reminiscence. "I think he was on *everyone's* list!"

"He was definitely on mine," she said. "Most of mine for the entire 80s."

"It's been ages since I made a really high-end to-do list like that," I said. "I used to be such a dreamer."

"Me too," she said. "For the last twenty or thirty years, my to-do lists have mainly included picking up cereal for the kids, signing school permissions, parent teacher nights, and doing laundry."

"Mine have been mainly getting work projects finished, contacting clients, developing marketing strategies for work, and all things problem solving," I said.

"Now we're just boring old fuddy-duddies," she said.

"*What?*" I asked in mock indignation. "Not *me!* Who knows, I could still be in a movie! It's never too late to be discovered! After all, wasn't Colonel Sanders something like a hundred when he invented chicken?"

We both laughed. "I think he was like 65," she corrected. "And he didn't *invent* chicken, it already existed."

"We should do it!" I said with a burst of inspiration.

"What? Invent chicken?" Frankie asked in shock.

"No, silly, be in a movie!" I said. "There are plenty of movies that get filmed right here in the city! We could easily become background actors! Think of all the stuff we know now that we didn't know then! I bet we *could* make all our dreams come true!"

"Do you really *think?*" she asked. "How could we *possibly* be in a movie?"

"Well, easy, we go online and register with a casting agency," I said. "Easy peasy. I'm not talking about becoming a major movie star. I just mean, you know, be an extra for a day or something so we can check it off our lists."

"Do you think?" she asked again, but her tone had a hint of belief in it this time.

"Of course!" I said. "Everything is figure-out-able!"

"It would help us earn money," she added slowly. "If we could do it, that is."

"Yes, that's right!" I agreed. I had no idea she was that worried about money. But she had mentioned that there was some glitch with her getting Edgar's benefits. "Think about it! We can do *anything* we want to! We have all the freedom we had when we were teenagers—and more! We have our own place, have knowledge we didn't have when we were younger, we have the internet, our kids are all adults, and we don't have stinky corporate jobs to tie us down!"

"You're *right!*" Frankie said with a touch of fire in her voice.

"You know what we need to do," I said.

"What?"

"*Make a list!*" I said, grabbing a pen from my desk drawer. "We've spent the past forty years following lists of stuff to do for other people, but we've never actually made a list that will make *us* happy!"

"That's true," she said. "If we could accomplish as

much as we have that we *didn't* want to do, I wonder what we can accomplish that we *do* want to do?"

"Exactly!" I said. "Time to make a list!"

"Yes! The best to-do list we've ever made!" she agreed.

"No, not a *to-do* list," I said. "A *Never-Got-To-Do* list!"

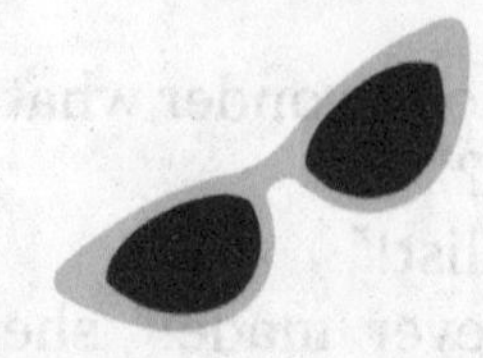

Chapter 7: The List

We started the list right after supper.

"Okay, here's what we have so far," I said, and re-capped our list thus far.

- Be in a movie
- Date a celebrity
- Ride in a limo
- Walk the red carpet
- Go on a cruise
- Sign autographs
- Publish a book
- Go on vacation in Hawaii
- Stay in a luxury hotel

"We can add more as we think of them," I said, and Frankie agreed.

"Where do we even begin?" she asked, and her tone told me she really didn't believe we could accomplish any of these, so I knew the first thing on my to-do list was to prove to her that we could. I'd have to start with the most doable.

"Well, first let's see what movies are being filmed around this city this summer," I said. I knew they filmed every summer and fall because the most scenic streets were blocked off by film crews a few times each year. Davenport wasn't Hollywood by any stretch of the imagination, but we only needed to be extras in a movie for one day for it to count!

My online search showed quite a few movies were scheduled to film in the area over the next few months, so my next search was to find out how to insert myself as an extra. I found a background casting agency that had online registrations, so we set up our accounts. Next, we felt like movie stars as we took each other's headshots against the white bathroom door. Neither of us were thrilled about having to take full body shots.

"I don't know if we should do this," Frankie said when we were filling out our applications. "I don't know what my measurements are." She blushed and her red face told me she *knew* what her measurements were. Just as I knew what mine were—well, vaguely—and I wasn't proud of mine either!

"Look, they don't really *care* what our measurements are," I told her. "This is just so that if they have to give us wardrobe, it has to fit exactly right or it costs them more money." I was basically regurgitating what I'd just read online, but it seemed to make her feel better. "And don't worry, I'm not anxious to find out what *my* exact measurements are either!"

With measured bravery, we retrieved a measuring tape from the craft room and soon had filled in the blanks with our embarrassing numbers.

"Well, maybe we should go on a diet first and try it in a few months," Frankie suggested. "After we've lost weight."

"Look, Frankie," I said, deciding it was time to get real with her. "If I wait until I'm *perfect* to live my life, I'll never get *anything* done at all! I haven't lost any weight in the last fifteen years, so I'm not going to put my life on hold any longer. I'm going to live *now*, and my body will get on board eventually."

She looked at me in awe like I was the bravest person on earth, but I wasn't. I was just tired of not living life to the fullest because I was embarrassed by a few extra pounds around my middle.

And then we waited. The following day we received an approval email and were told to check the website each day for upcoming gigs and select any we wanted. They would notify us if we were chosen.

"Well, we're available for all of them," I said and clicked them off. There were only three upcoming ones. One was for a commercial being filmed in a larger city an hour away, and the other two were for a series that was being filmed in Davenport for the summer and fall. The series was a mystery series.

We never did hear back about the commercial, but within a few days, we received emails asking us to confirm our availability for two full days the following week for background acting on the series, Detective Jones.

"Oh, this is so exciting!" I said, feeling like I was twenty again. "I can't believe we're going to be on TV!"

"I know, I can't either!" Frankie said with the same excitement she used to have when we were young!

"We're gonna be on TV!" I said. "Like movie stars!"

"Like TV stars anyway," she said. "And I've never even watched the show!"

"Me neither!" I said. "Let's see if we can find it streaming online somewhere."

"It should be on *actual* TV!" she said.

"This calls for a celebration!" I said and ran for the tub of chocolate ice cream in the freezer.

"Yes!" she said. "I'll check the TV guide to see when and where it comes on!" She rushed for the TV, bouncing along the way while I grabbed bowls for ice cream.

"Oh, I need to tell someone!" I said. "I'm calling Jetta!"

So, I called my daughter, and Frankie called her son to share the exciting news. I was sure Tommy would be happy to learn his mother was beginning to live life again.

Jetta was just as thrilled for me. "Oh, that is *so* *exciting*, Mom!" she said. "I can't wait to tell David! He watches that show every week!"

I felt more alive with each passing moment. I was sure Frankie felt the same.

"It was much easier than I thought," I said. "You know, honey, about that whole grave thing."

"Mom, I already said I'm sorry!" she said with a groan. I instantly felt like an idiot for ruining a joyful moment.

"I know, I'm just saying, you should really return it and get your money back," I said. "You should use the money for yourself and the kids. That's what your dad would've wanted."

"I don't want to talk about this anymore, Mom!" she said. "I don't care what Dad would've wanted. The only thing *he* ever wanted was what *he* wanted. He never cared about you or me!"

"Honey, that's not true," I said. "But I'm sorry I brought it up." Her unexpected attitude was bringing *me* down, and I'd expected to at least be able to ride this happiness train well into the following week.

"Listen, I didn't want the money, and I don't want it back," she said. "But I'll return it and give the money to *you*. The quicker I don't have to deal with that entire thing anymore, the better. I have a new baby on the way, and I just want to be happy and focus on that. I want to focus on new life, not death and graves."

"Okay, two things, and then I'll let it go," I said. "One, *you* are the one that bought my grave, not me. Two, *now* you know how *I* feel. I may be old, but I'm not over the hill yet. I just want to focus on life, not death."

She was silent for a moment. "Okay," she said. "I'll return it and get the money back and give it to you. Take it and go on an adventure or something."

I felt awkward about taking the money from her, especially not knowing how much money it was. I would put it in an account and worry about it later.

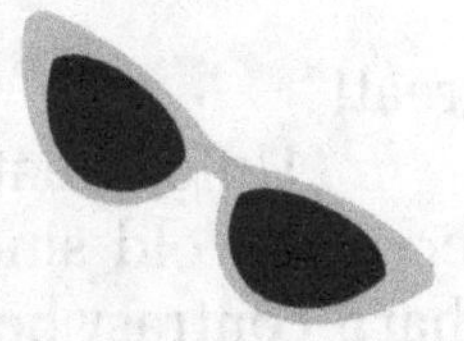

Chapter 8: The Show

Frankie and I spent the entire rest of the week binge watching Detective Jones.

"We're going to be working with *Darwin Beckett!*" she squealed during every commercial.

"*I know!*" I said. We'd been fans of his since the 80s and watched him move from teen heartthrob roles to adult heartthrob roles. Despite the fact we were born the same year, he looked nearly half my age. Men age differently.

After the ice cream celebration of our new gigs, we swore off the ice cream. That was mainly Frankie's idea. "I don't want Darwin Beckett to see me like *this!*"

"Well, I don't want him to see me like this either," I said. "But I doubt I can accomplish in five days what I couldn't do in the past fifteen years." And I indulged in slightly less ice cream than usual.

We dyed our hair with boxes of youthful brown that we bought at the drug store. It was messy and I ended up with spots on my ears that I hoped I could scrub off before the big day. In the end I had to cover them with makeup. We were told not to wash our hair on the day of the filming because it would be too shiny on TV.

"I think we look fine," I said, despite my ears, as we evaluated our dye job in the bathroom mirror.

"Well, now I look too pale," Frankie said. "I think it makes me look older."

"We just have to add makeup," I said. "We'll be

great!"

Unfortunately, the only makeup I owned was about ten years old since I wore it so sparingly, and with the sharp contrast between my newly darkened hair and my paler skin, my drugstore makeup looked too pink, and it was impossible to look good.

"I think we look like clowns," Frankie said.

"We just need to invest in better quality makeup," I said. "These are old and out of style. Besides, there are girls at the drugstore that can help us pick out the right shades and stuff."

On Tuesday night we kept checking our emails and at 10 p.m., our call sheets came in.

"Our very first *call sheets!*" I squealed.

"I feel like a *real* movie star!" Frankie was enthused. "Look! There are our names!"

"And the name and logo of the show!" I pointed it out in excitement. "Proof we did this!"

"We need to start a scrapbook!" Frankie said. "Just like the old days!"

"Yes!" I agreed. "And we can chart every success on our list!"

By Wednesday at four in the morning, we were in too much of a rush in leaving the apartment to be able to worry about makeup. The main thing we remembered from all the read and reread emails was not to show up late to set!

When we arrived at the studio, a big square building on the edge of the city, we were directed to a large room with a sign that said BG *Holding Area.* A young guy with a headset on rushed through an introduction. All I got out of his rapid sentence was that his name was Mark something and he was some kind of AD. First or Second AD. I was so excited to just be there that I couldn't pay attention. He ushered us into the room which had cafeteria style rows of tables.

Frankie and I sat at the one nearest the door. There were already a few people sitting at some of the other tables, and I discovered a sense of shyness that I hadn't felt since high school. It surprised me, but my excitement over being in *Detective Jones* wasn't about to be quashed by a little high school shyness. The room gradually filled up and a few more people sat down at our table.

"Is this your first time?" asked a sharp-looking gentleman about our age with flecks of gray in his short hair. He had classic Hollywood style looks, and I felt a little in awe of him.

"Yes," I said and introduced Frankie and me. He told us his name was Carl.

"I've been doing this for about three years now," he said. "Oh, here's Susan, she's an oldie too!" I wasn't sure if he was calling us *oldies* because of our age, or if he meant he and Susan were both regular extras.

Susan sat down, and we introduced ourselves again. I was pleased that both Carl and Susan were around our age, proving that we were *not* too old to do this.

"I'm so excited!" I confessed, mainly because I just couldn't hold it in any longer, and it was so thrilling to be with some like-minded people.

"It's fun," Carl agreed. "Sure beats working at the car factory!"

It was at that moment that we were interrupted by someone who was in charge of something.

"Hey, everyone, I'm Paul," he said. He was some sort of AD and ran us through the rules: no whispering on set, silent mouth movements only; no phones, cameras, or pictures; and never to approach the main actors on set.

I nodded so hard my neck ached. *No way was I*

messing this up!

"And, for any of you who are new," Paul said, looking straight at me. Probably because I was still nodding. "Don't forget to register with Stan at the back of the room." As soon as he left, Frankie and I were the only ones that got up to go back and register, so clearly, we were the only newbies there.

"How has this kind of opportunity been under our noses for so long and we had absolutely no idea?" I whispered to her.

"Well, I've been living under a rock for forty years, so *I* can't really be blamed," she said.

Yeah, but what was my excuse? I'd lived in Davenport for years, yet I'd never even thought to pursue anything beyond a corporate job. I'd been missing out on these kinds of opportunities just because I'd been distracted with other jobs that had only caused stress. From my calculations, I would make at least $200 for the day if we stayed until five. To think I could've been doing *this* for a career—what an eye opener.

We registered and sat down. I was too nervous to eat anything from the breakfast food tray, but Carl and Susan had donuts. Frankie seemed to give up on worrying about her weight and did the same.

They delivered small slips of paper with the scenes on that we were doing that day. "Those are called sides," Carl pointed out. "It's just the scenes we'll be involved in. The ones that have Xs through them they aren't filming today."

"Okay, thanks," I said, appreciating the help from a seasoned background performer.

Wardrobe girls came in with clothes and purses for us to try on. I was able to stick with my current jeans and blouse and they just gave me a suit jacket to wear over it.

Frankie got a sweater and a handbag.

The hair and makeup ladies brushed and styled our hair, right in the background holding room, and applied makeup for us, which was a relief because I didn't want to go on TV looking like a clown, which would've likely been the case had I done my own makeup.

Frankie was so nervous she had to go to the bathroom about six times, and I had to go with her because she was shy. I just used the time to look at my new Hollywood self in the mirror; I was not using a public bathroom unless I absolutely *had* to.

Finally, that Mark guy came in and pointed to Frankie, Carl and me. "You three, come," he said, and we instantly got up and followed him down the hall to the heavily anticipated set.

My mind raced, and I looked over at Frankie who clearly was dealing with the same racing thoughts. *I can't believe we're being called to set! I'm going to be on set! On set! I've made it now!*

Not to mention the thoughts about being within ten feet of *Darwin Beckett!*

A few more background actors trickled down behind us as a second group of choices. A sturdy woman with a belt of leather pockets and a Walkie-Talkie in her hand and a headset on came over and touched me on the shoulder. "You, come with me," she said. "And you." I was relieved to see she'd picked Frankie too.

We followed her over to a corporate waiting room area, which was so realistic, I had flashbacks of my last corporate job. The floors, marble-lined corridors, and waiting room, complete with a receptionist's desk and elevator doors—which I learned later were pulled open with ropes from behind—were indistinguishable from the real thing. Frankie sat beside me, and I reached out and clutched her hand. She squeezed back and we exchanged a knowing silent smile.

The director and others walked back and forth, explaining the scene to the actors, and then the main cast arrived—including Darwin Beckett! I shot Frankie another glance and we both silently screamed with our eyes.

Darwin was just as handsome as when he was young. I couldn't believe I was only about twelve feet away from him. A large camera and a group of people were just beyond the edge of the receptionist's desk, enveloped in darkness. A guy brought a couple other background actors over to stand behind Frankie and me, and I heard him instruct them how to stand and pretend like they're talking.

"Okay, you two," he said as he came around and faced us. "This girl over here will come over and sit down and pretend to talk to you guys. Just pretend you're having a conversation with her. The director will call 'background' and that's when you guys start acting, got it?"

We both nodded.

Everyone got in position. The Assistant Directors took scripts from the main actors and left the set, and soon Frankie and I were just left sitting in the empty corporate waiting area. The AD came over to us again.

"Okay, listen, you two come with me," he led us back to the hallway area of the set. "When he calls 'background', you two walk from here over to those seats where you were, and then the other girl will come over, okay?"

We nodded and stood in the fake corridor. I was still amazed at how realistic everything was. It was like they'd plucked up a corporate office right out of the real world.

"Quiet on set!" The director called. "Sound! Camera! Background!"

I started walking. I'd taken two steps when the director called, "Action!" It confused me, and I thought maybe I wasn't supposed to have started walking yet. I stopped and when everyone else began moving I turned and headed straight for the seats. Frankie was behind me.

"Cut!" The director yelled. "Back to first position!"

We went back over to the wall, and the woman with the Walkie-Talkie came to me. "When he yells background, start walking to the chairs," she said. "He'll call action for the main actors."

Was it my fault they'd had to cut?

"Quiet on set!" The director called. "Sound! Camera! Background!"

I started walking much more naturally to the chairs this time instead of rushing like I had the first time. *I guess it had been my fault they'd called cut.*

"Action!"

By then I'd almost reached the chairs, and as we sat down, a guy in a business suit walked down to the receptionist's desk and pretended to have a conversation with the young woman. A couple other background actors walked up the hallway. Darwin Beckett walked down the hallway towards the elevator, and the elevator door slid open and a woman, the other main character and Detective Jones's love interest, stepped out of the elevator. They said their lines, but they talked in low tones, which surprised me because I figured they would speak louder. But with the boom mic being held just above their heads, I guess it didn't matter that they were just talking normally. I was also surprised that the set wasn't brightly lit. It seemed like any ordinary room.

After several more takes, we had lunch, which I was too excited to eat, but Frankie wasn't.

"Why aren't you eating?" she asked as she shoveled spaghetti into her mouth.

"You know I can't eat when I'm nervous," I reminded her.

"Still?" she asked with her eyes bulging in shock and her cheeks bulging in spaghetti.

"I may look older," I said. "But my personality hasn't aged a bit." I wanted to tell her that hers apparently hadn't either because she always ate when she was nervous or depressed.

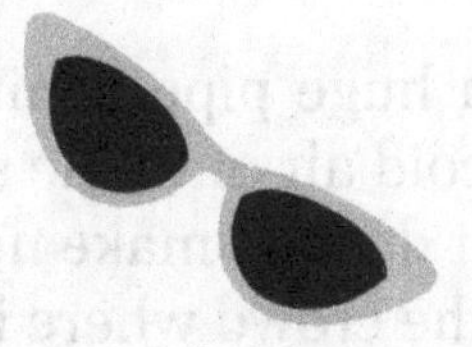

Chapter 9: Seeing Stars

After lunch, it was time to film the warehouse scene. It was only my second time being ushered to a set, but I felt that it was a milestone. *Going to set once is something you've done; twice makes it something you do!*

This time Frankie and I were part of a crowd standing in a warehouse listening to a dire speech by Detective Jones—*the one and only Darwin Beckett!* Frankie and I maneuvered through the crowd so we could be at the front. I was going to be mere inches from him—and a fake dead man! *But* mere *inches!*

We had to stand a long time and as more background actors were brought in, Darwin and his female counterpart sat on chairs and whispered and giggled. I tried not to stare but, come on, it was *Darwin Beckett!* The guy pretending to be dead didn't get off the floor, but he did lean on his elbows and join in the whispered hilarity with his co-stars.

After standing so long that my back was starting to hurt, and my legs were getting tired, the filming finally began. It was so hot and felt like it was growing hotter by the second. The camera was moved to the front of the crowd and the scene was filmed again and again.

"It is so hot in here," I whispered to Carl who stood on the other side of me.

"Air conditioning makes too much noise so they can't have it on set," he whispered back. "But they have a huge pipe behind that fake wall back there that blows cold air onto the set. That way there is a little cool air, but it doesn't make noise. Maybe you should go to the back of the crowd where it's cooler."

"No, I was already filmed standing here so I don't want to mess up the scene and get in trouble," I said. And there is no way I'm going to go through all this and hide myself in the back where Darwin Beckett can't even see me!

So, the minutes dragged on. The scene was shot again and again *and again*. Finally, I could no longer hide my discomfort. Sweat was pouring down my temples and I only hoped it couldn't be seen on camera. When the director called action, I was ready to fall. I could feel my heart racing in my chest, and I hoped this wasn't a heart attack or something. Sweat beaded on my forehead, and I felt weak. The director called "Cut!" and I heard someone say, "She's gonna faint!"

I turned to try and take up that offer of moving to the back, but it was too late, and I felt my knees buckle as a strong grip on either forearm whisked me off set.

"Are you okay?" The woman with the Walkie-Talkies asked me as someone produced a chair under me.

"Yes, I'm fine," I said, although clearly, I was not. "It is so hot in there!"

"Yes," they both said.

"Go get a wet cloth!" the woman ordered Mark, and he trotted off down the hall.

"What happened to you?" A woman that had been sitting at our table in the holding room asked as she was walking towards the set.

"I fainted," I said.

"I'll go get her some water," she said and hurried off, returning quickly with a bottle of cool water.

"Thank you so much," I said. "I'm so embarrassed."

"Don't worry," the Walkie-Talkie woman said. "This happens all the time. Everyone has fainted on set at some point."

The producer and director came out to see if I was okay and introduced themselves. I was so amazed that the *producer and director* were speaking to me that I didn't quite catch their names. Plus, my head was still kind of woozy.

"I'm good now," I said. "I can go back in."

"You have to wait until the medic sees you," the producer said. "Just wait here."

He and the director left.

"Hey there," another guy said, coming up to me with a medical bag. "I'm Eric, the medic. Is it okay if I take your blood pressure?"

"Yes, of course, but I'm feeling much better now," I said. "It was just really hot in there."

He took my blood pressure, and it was fine. *At least I think it was fine.* He didn't specifically *say* it was fine. "Did you eat lunch?" he asked.

"To be honest, I skipped lunch," I said. "I was too excited to eat."

He smiled. "Well, I'm also with craft services, too," he said. "Would you like me to make you a sandwich?"

"I'm fine really," I insisted. *I was so embarrassed.*

"I think it would help if you ate something," he urged. "Why don't you let me make you a chicken sandwich?"

"Okay, sure," I finally agreed. "Thank you. But I'm fine, honestly."

"And, Nancy, why don't you take her outside for some fresh air?" He said.

He left and Nancy, the woman with the Walkie-Talkie, took my arm and helped me up as Mark finally returned with a cold wet paper towel.

"Sorry," he said. "This was all I could find."

He put it on my forehead, and it *did* feel good. I thanked him, and holding the paper towel to my forehead, I went outside with Nancy. I was surprised that my knees still felt a bit wobbly.

She led me to a bench, and I sat down. She sat beside me.

"I'm sorry for being such a bother," I said. "I should've moved to the back of the room by the air vent earlier."

"No, don't worry about it," she said. "It's a rite of passage. It happens to everyone."

She sat with me until Eric returned with my sandwich.

"Can you stay with her?" Nancy asked. "I have to get back to set."

"Sure," Eric said.

She left and shortly after, the guy that had been holding the boom mic came out. "Hey, I came out to see if you're okay," the guy said. "I'm Jack."

"Hi, I'm Del," I said. "I'm doing much better."

"That's good to hear," he said. "Hey, don't feel bad. I fainted my first time on set too."

I smiled. I thought it was kind that everyone told me that. *It must be true.*

After he left because he had to go back to set, I tried to focus on eating the sandwich.

"Can I get you anything else?" Eric asked. "Would you like a blanket?"

"No, I'm fine, really," I said.

"I need to check your pulse again, if that's okay," he said. I held out my wrist and he checked my pulse.

"We'll just sit out here a little while longer," he said.

"I feel bad that I'm taking up your time," I said. "I'm sure you have other stuff you need to be doing."

"*This is* what I'm supposed to be doing," he said. "Don't worry."

And then—*and then*—something unbelievable happened. The door opened and *Darwin Beckett stepped out!*

"Hey, I came out to see how you're doing," he said in his smooth style that I'd idolized for much of my life.

"I'm fine," I said, although now I felt even more shaky. *The* Darwin Beckett had purposedly come out to see if I was okay!

"I can sit with her for a while if you need me to," Darwin said.

"Okay, I'll be right back," Eric said. "I'm going to get her another sandwich."

"I'm fine, really," I said for the hundredth time.

Eric left and Darwin *sat down beside me!*

"I fainted *my* first time on set," Darwin said with a grin. "I was so embarrassed. I'm sure by now a dozen people have said that to you. Everyone faints on set the first day. I've even seen cameramen, and even directors, faint their first day."

"Wow, really?" I asked. *I had never thought of that.* "Maybe that should be included in the list of great expectations for beginners."

"You have a great sense of humor," Darwin said. "Is this your first time acting?"

"Well, I wouldn't call what *I* was doing *acting,*" I said. "More like falling."

He chuckled again. "Background acting is still acting," he said. "How realistic would any movie or show be if there were no background actors? Just picture it. If only the main characters were the only ones in a diner, or a hospital, or a concert. None of it would be believable to the audience. Background actors are the most important actors on set. They are what make the audience suspend their disbelief."

"Wow, I never thought of it like that," I said. I couldn't believe it! Darwin Beckett—*the real Darwin Beckett*—was actually sitting next to me! Casually chatting like it was no big deal! Meanwhile, I was busy trying not to faint again from sheer disbelief!

"So, other than, you know, the falling part, what do you think of your first day on set?" he asked.

"I'm amazed," I told him. "It's unbelievable how realistic the set is!"

"I know," he said. "The hammers do an amazing job!"

"Hammers?"

"That's what we call the set builders," he said. "They are the unsung heroes of every production."

Nancy came and poked her head out the door. "Dar, they need you on set."

"Okay," he said, and turned to me. "You take care, now. Eric will be back in a second."

Nancy came out and Darwin left and then Eric returned with another sandwich.

"There you are!" Frankie came out the door. "I was *so* worried! What happened to you?"

"I'm fine," I said.

Eric gave me the sandwich, checked my pulse again, and then told me to wrap out for the day.

So, I walked back to the holding room with Frankie and told Stan, or whatever his name was at the back table that Eric said to wrap out." He signed his name to a card, stamped the time on it and handed it to me and got me to sign a piece of paper.

"You won't believe what happened!" I said as soon as I sat back down beside Frankie.

"What?"

"Darwin Beckett came out to ask how I was doing!" I whispered. I didn't want to seem like such a fan girl to other background actors coming into the room. "He sat beside me, and we had a conversation!"

"No way!" she said. "I don't believe you!"

"Seriously!" I said. "Would I lie about that?"

"He was on set the entire time!" she said. "There's no way that could happen! Maybe you hit your head and hallucinated it!"

"I know what happened!" I said, offended that she didn't believe me. *Why would I lie to my best friend?* Her look remained skeptical.

"I saw the guy sitting beside you and it wasn't Darwin; it was the medic," she said.

"I know and he's also with craft services," I said. "And his name is Eric." *I threw in his name to prove I knew him better than she did.* "Plus, I met the producer and director!"

"Right," she said. "Why would the producer and director go outside to meet you?"

"They didn't go outside," I said. "They introduced themselves to me in the hallway."

She rolled her eyes which ticked me off.

"Why on earth would I lie?" I asked her.

"Fine," she said. "I believe you."

But she sure didn't sound like she did!

Chapter 10: The Set – Day 2

The following day, the novelty of getting up at 4 a.m. had worn off, and I crawled into the same jeans and blouse I wore the day before. They had stressed that we were to wear the same clothes for continuity.

"I wish I'd worn my more comfortable clothes yesterday," Frankie mumbled as she climbed into the car. We'd made it a habit for me to pick her up out front so that she wouldn't have to go near the storage room and deal with sad memories. I was tired from waking up so early, still annoyed about her not believing me the day before about me meeting Darwin Beckett, and envious of her privilege of just having to go to the lobby and wait while I had to make one extra stop before getting on our way. Even *I* knew this pettiness was more about her having the audacity to insinuate that I would lie to her about *anything*, than the actual effort to just put on the brakes for a few seconds for her to get into the car.

I didn't speak to Frankie in the holding room, mainly because I was exhausted, not upset with her. She obviously took it as me being mad, so she made a point of engaging in a nonstop conversation with Carl.

This time, I didn't skip breakfast. I did not want to faint again. Although, the thought of another personal encounter with Darwin Beckett made the idea of fainting surprisingly appealing. After downing several blueberry muffins and a coffee, I brushed my teeth and felt a bit more alive.

After hair, makeup and wardrobe, we were called to set to finish the warehouse scene. I was glad that I'd been in the front the day before because, for continuity, we had to stand in the same places. I was glad Frankie was on the other side of Carl because I was still a little annoyed with her. The crew came in and the boom mic guy, whose name I'd already forgotten, came in and climbed up on a stepladder while the mic was adjusted.

"I didn't expect to see *you* here today," he said with a wide grin.

"The show must go on!" I replied enthusiastically. "If I pass out again today, just drag me over by that other dead guy, and Detective Jones can call me victim number two!"

He laughed.

Then the actors took their places and scanned their lines while cameras and lights were adjusted. I couldn't help but stare at Darwin. I was surprised when he looked up from his paper and smiled at me. Then, as if the gods of fortune all got together and smiled down on me at once, *he began walking towards me! This was it! It was happening! Right now! In public!*

I glanced over at Frankie to see if she was looking. *Of course she was looking.* Most of the female background actors had their eyes constantly glued on Darwin Beckett!

"How are you feeling today?" he asked me in a low tone.

"I'm feeling much better," I said. "And thank you so much for coming out to see how I was yesterday. That was so kind of you."

"That was no problem," he said with a smile. "I'm glad you're feeling better today."

"Thank you," I said. My brain screamed at me to

say something clever. Something that would make him remember me forever, but all I managed to do was to smile like an idiot. *Darwin Beckett had actually been thinking about me! He must've been thinking about me last night wondering if I was okay. Imagine! He was actually concerned about me!*

He turned and walked back to his spot with his co-stars, and I turned to look at Frankie to make sure she saw *that* encounter. She had! And her expression of amazement and envy was priceless.

"You know Darwin Beckett?" Another background actor standing just behind me whispered in my ear.

I wanted so much to say yes, but I was afraid he would be able to hear me, so I just whispered back, "Not really."

It wasn't just that I'd been enamored with Darwin Beckett since I was like *twelve,* but now I had so much respect for him as a *person.* He was truly kind to take the time to ask me how I was. I was more impressed with him than I'd ever been before.

At the end of the day, Frankie and I drove home, tired and happy and two hundred dollars richer.

"I'm so sorry I didn't believe you," Frankie said. "I just *couldn't believe it.* I thought you hit your head when you fell and were hallucinating. Honestly, that's what I thought."

"First of all, I didn't fall," I clarified. "I was *about* to fall, and Nancy and Mark grabbed me and helped me out. Weren't you watching?"

"I didn't know anything was happening until they were carrying you out," she said. "And who's Nancy?"

"The woman with the Walkie-Talkie," I said.

"Okay, okay," she said. "Maybe I shouldn't have doubted you, but let's just say you've been known to embellish a thing or two! I should've known only *you* can turn a health crisis into a glamorous movie star encounter."

We both laughed because it was true. I somehow *did* have a knack for turning disasters into opportunities.

"Well, at least we accidentally found a great way to supplement our incomes!" I enthused. "Let's go out and celebrate!"

So, we went out for burgers and fries again. Our Hollywood roles were done for the time being, so it wasn't like we had to be concerned about calories for the day.

It was with great pride that we checked off *Be in a movie*. It wasn't a *movie*, but it still counted. It was a TV show. We'd still acted in *something!* Plus, Darwin Beckett had told me how important my role really was, so *that* made it count!

Chapter 11: Grave Returns

"Now what should we tackle?" Frankie asked me as soon as I got up. She was still in her husband's pajamas and staring at our list pinned to the living room wall. "Since you've already become friends with Darwin Beckett, if you date him, you can check off *date a celebrity*."

"Okay, first of all, he's married," I said. "So, no."

"Well, if we keep doing this show, maybe we can get to know some of the other actors," she suggested.

"I don't know about you," I said as I poured coffee, "but getting up at four in the morning isn't something I'm going to be able to maintain."

"Yeah," she agreed. "I think I was asleep before I was even in bed last night."

"I think I'm too old to do that on an ongoing basis," I said. It wasn't that I was lazy, but that I knew the value of a good night's sleep. "I've spent forty years getting up to alarm clocks to show up for work, and I don't want to spend my golden years continuing to do that. In fact, if we could find the money, I'd like to focus on taking a cruise next!"

"Well, it would have to be a pretty cheap cruise," she said. "The only extra money we've made is $400 each."

"Well, I have an idea," I said. "How much do you think a grave costs?"

"*What?*" she shrieked. "What are you thinking?" In my head I visualized six question marks after her question.

"No, whatever it is you *think* I'm thinking, I'm not," I said with a laugh. "Jetta bought a grave and tombstone for me."

"What?" she shrieked again. "Why would you want that?" I could see the idea of death and graves was still touchy for her—and I should've known better—but I wasn't thinking about the fact that she was still wearing her husband's pajamas and considering him to be living in the garage.

"Well, I didn't exactly *ask* her to do it," I pointed out. "It was more of an ongoing feud between her and her neighbor than anything personal about *me*. And let's just say, I was surprised when *I* found out!" I shut up to prevent myself from going down a morbid rabbit hole by pointing out that it would probably be of use *someday*. I knew that D word was still off limits for her.

"Still, that was insensitive of her," she said. "I mean, to buy it without even *asking* you first."

"*Again,*" I said. "Her heart was in the right place. She thought she was doing the right thing."

"I suppose," she said. "I *still* can't believe you let your husband name her after his car!"

It was time to confess. "Okay, look, I'll tell you something if you swear you will never breathe a word of it to Jetta," I said. Only after she nodded and promised and crossed her heart, I divulged the truth. "I know Fred joked he named her after his car, but *he* wasn't the one that named her Jetta."

"What?" Frankie stared at me like she was questioning everything she ever knew about me.

"It was an *accident,*" I said. "It was only hours after she was born, and I was kind of out of it. When the nurse brought me in a form to fill out for parking—since my car was going to be there for a couple days—she set it on top of the registration form. Anyway, when I was writing in the type of car we had, I accidentally wrote it on the birth registration as her given name. Fred was thrilled with it when he found out because it *was* true, he *did* love our car."

"Wow," was all she could say.

"We always told Jetta that we named her after the gemstone, Jet, which symbolizes elegance, strength and beauty and is supposed to have protective properties," I said. "I had to look it up because I never wanted her to think she was named after a car. Although that's what Fred always joked about, it was never true."

"Why not just tell her the truth?" Frankie asked. "It's not like she's a kid anymore."

"I will someday," I said. "If the subject ever comes up—and if she ever develops a sense of humor."

"So, what are you going to do with the . . . you know what?" she asked.

"Well, I made it clear that I don't want it, and I have no intention of spending the rest of my life, er *afterlife,* lying next to *that* old cheater," I said, carefully avoiding the word *death*. "And she doesn't want that other woman to have it for some reason, so she's going to return it, get her money back, and she insists on giving the money to me."

"Oh, well, I have no idea what that would cost," she said, which shocked me because her husband had just . . . moved to the afterlife!

"But didn't," I began. "I mean, . . . you know, *Edgar.*"

"Tommy handled everything," she said. The look of sadness on her face told me that I'd just accidentally swept her into the past again.

"So," I said brightly. "I'll look it up and see how much we can expect to get for it, and then it might be enough for us to take a cruise!"

"No, let's just do background acting until we save up enough money," Frankie insisted. "I'd rather do that."

Her serious look made it clear she wanted absolutely nothing to do with anything involving my grave, including the selling of it. I was hoping she'd be recovering by now, but it was clear she was going to take a much longer time to get over her husband. I considered suggesting therapy to her because her mood was sinking right before my very eyes, and despite being a competent problem-solver, I was nowhere near equipped to help my best friend.

"Okay, let's see what else is on the list," I said, going back to the board. It seemed to be the only thing that brightened her up, so I was going to milk that for all it was worth. "Maybe we can even add some new things to it. What else have we never got to do, that we can possibly afford to do with $400?"

Before we had a chance to add anything else, my door buzzer sounded. It was Jetta. "Come on up," I said and buzzed her in.

"Oh, I better go get dressed!" Frankie said as she shuffled into the bedroom and closed the door just before Jetta knocked.

"It's almost noon, Mom!" Jetta said with a look of shock as soon as she walked into my apartment. "Why aren't you dressed?"

"I slept in," I admitted. "Turns out show business is a lot of work!"

"Oh yeah, how did your great acting experience turn out?" she asked.

"I made $400 and got to meet a celebrity," I said proudly—purposely leaving out the part about me fainting. "The episode will air sometime in late November. So, to what do I owe this surprise visit? Are you still checking up on me?"

"No, Mom," she said as Frankie came out of the bedroom, all dressed. "Oh, hi, Mrs. Krane!"

"Oh, call me Aunt Frankie, dear," Frankie said. "Your mom is like a sister to me!"

"Okay, Aunt Frankie," Jetta said with a laugh. "How do you like living in the city?"

"Let's just say every day with your mother is an adventure," she said.

"Don't I know it!" Jetta agreed, and they both laughed.

"I can't help it if I'm the most exciting person you both know!" I said brightly, but inside I was insulted. *They act like being fun is a crime!* "So, Jetta, how did selling off the grave plot and tombstone go?"

"Well, I'll leave you two to visit," Frankie said abruptly. "I'm going to go for a walk and enjoy this beautiful day!" She had her purse in hand and shoes on within sixty seconds and was out the door, waving her keys.

"What's wrong with her?" Jetta asked.

"Her husband died two years ago, and she doesn't want to hear me talk about graves," I said, ashamed of myself for my attitude but finding it harder to control my tolerance for being laughed at right to my face. "Anyway, did you get rid of that grave?"

"No," she said flatly and pulled a thick envelope out of her purse as she sat down on the sofa. "The guy said he's never had a grave returned before and had no way to process a refund. Obviously, he just didn't *want* to, considering all he had to do was reverse the charges."

"Well, I guess it would be unusual for someone to return a grave," I said. "But I'm surprised it doesn't happen more often if he pushes people to buy graves in advance!"

"Well, turns out he overcharged for it because Mrs. Ross and I were having a bidding war for the last plot, so he raised the price. Now he refuses to take it back," she said. "So here, this is all the paperwork, it has your name on it as the owner, and it belongs to you. If you can resell it, maybe you can get at least half of the money back. What he used as a selling point is that it overlooks the water."

"Why pay extra for a grave overlooking the water when I can take the money and overlook the water while I'm alive?" I said. I opened the envelope and was shocked at what she'd paid. *"Eight thousand dollars?"*

"Like I said, it overlooks the water and there was a bidding war," she said. "And he threw in a free casket to sweeten the deal."

"This is an awful lot of money," I said, still staring at the receipt. "Are you sure you don't want this money back if I can sell it? I mean, you guys are having another baby; how can you turn down money like this?"

"Mom, David owns a business, and I do software programming from home," she said. "We are not hurting for money. And besides, I've already told you, this just feels like dirty money to me."

"Well, you bought me a *grave*, for Pete's sake!" I said. "But money is still money. It's a tool, and it's all about how you use it. If you honestly don't want it, I will certainly put it to good use!"

"Please, Mom, take it with my blessing!" she said, shoving my hand away from her for emphasis.

As soon as Jetta left, I called every funeral home in the city. I wanted to get this sold before Frankie returned and freaked out because I was dealing with graves, caskets, and tombstones. When none of the funeral homes I called were willing to pay my price, I turned to the online marketplace. To take Frankie on a cruise, I figured I would need at least $10,000. But since the plot had been overpriced to begin with—and no one apparently saw the value in spending eternity next to my cheating ex-husband—the only offers I could get for the entire bundle were between $2000 to $4000, and that just wouldn't do.

And then, after only two hours, I had a message from an interested buyer. After a phone call to verify the person was legitimately interested and not some axe murderer that figured I was a prime target because I came with my own grave, I was satisfied. She was a nice lady who was fulfilling her mother's wish to be buried in that exact spot because it was beside her soulmate. How touching. It was amazing how Fred had a family that didn't want to be beside him for eternity, and yet just on the other side of an empty plot, lay a man that a dying woman was willing to pay $10,000 to lie beside. I grabbed my purse and the thick envelope and headed out, leaving a note on the fridge for Frankie, simply stating that I had to run an errand. Turns out having the last spot in the center of a cemetery beside someone's soulmate was a hot commodity after all!

When I reached the garage, I was shocked to see the light on and the door ajar to the storage room. I cringed over my selfish insensitivity earlier and tapped on the door. "Frankie, are you in here?"

She was sitting cross-legged on the floor. She wasn't crying though. "What are you doing?" I asked.

"Just talking to Edgar," she said with a sigh.

Oh! I didn't realize she talked to him!

"I have to run an errand," I said. "I'll be back in a while."

"Where?" she asked. "I need to get out of this room. I've been sitting on this hard concrete floor for two hours! Mainly because I couldn't get up after the *first* hour. If you help me up, I'll go with you."

I was surprised by her willingness to leave Edgar.

"Um, well, okay," I said. I didn't have to divulge

where I was going, or what I was doing.

"Where are we going?" she asked as we got into the car.

I didn't want to lie. "I just have to go meet with someone," I said.

"Someone, who?" she asked, eyeing me suspiciously.

"Oh, it's just about something I sold on the marketplace," I said, carefully avoiding the full details.

"I hope it's that stupid grave you're selling!" she said.

"It is!" I said, shocked and relieved at the same time.

"Good!" she said. "I can't stand the thought that you're preparing for your death!"

Death? "You said the D word!" I said.

"Yeah, because the word doesn't mean anything if you're still alive!" she said. "I've lost enough people, Del. I can't bear the thought of losing you too! The quicker you can get rid of that, the better!"

I smiled. Frankie was complex. I'd forgotten that about her. "Well, you're not going to lose me that easily!" I said. "We've got too much living to do before either of us has to worry about that ever again!"

And it was a promise I intended to keep!

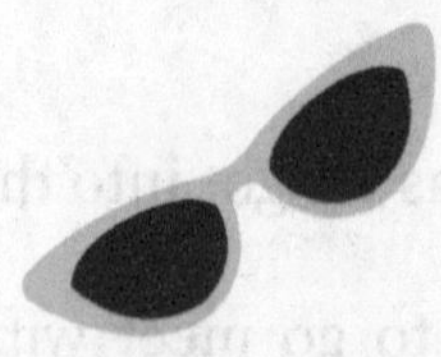

Chapter 12: First Class and a Hole in the Ground

The extra $10,000 made me feel like we'd won the lottery, and we celebrated with junk food and ice cream (which counts as dairy, so *not* junk food), and browsed the internet for hours looking for good deals on cruises.

"Oh . . . my . . .gosh!" Frankie said slowly as she stared at her laptop screen.

"What?" I looked up from my own screen. Her words were flat so I couldn't tell if it was a *good* oh-my-gosh or a bad oh-my-gosh.

"You are *never* going to believe who is hosting a cruise!" she said, and her voice rose to a squeak.

"Who?" I asked. I could already feel the stirring of excitement.

"Brake Caldwell!" she squealed. "Brake Caldwell! We *must* sign up for this cruise!"

I gasped. "Brake Caldwell? As in *the* Brake Caldwell? As in *kissing-his-posters-every-night-before-going-to-sleep Brake Caldwell?* That Brake Caldwell?"

"The one and only!" she said, spinning the screen so I could see.

There he was. *My* Brake Caldwell, smiling that million-dollar-smile that had stolen my heart back in 1985, still looking like a leading man. He was listed as the host of the Keto Cruise which promised eight luxurious days on the ocean and three luxurious nights in Hawaii.

"Hootin' banana crackers! We *have* to go!" I said firmly. "How much is it? Hurry, book it!"

"You do it!" she insisted. "It's *your* money!"

She sent me the link, and I quickly registered. "It's not that expensive," I said. "Not when you consider it's all inclusive. Plus, it includes three days in *Hawaii!*"

"*Hawaii!*" she shouted. "That's on our list!"

"And look," I said. "Includes luxury hotel rooms for the three nights in Hawaii!"

"And *that's* on our list!"

"We are doing it, Frankie!" I said. I felt like my insides were about to burst from excitement.

"I've never heard of the Keto Cruise Line," she said. "They must be new."

"Maybe that's why they're trying to get people to book by having a celebrity on it," I suggested.

"Probably," she agreed. "And maybe we can even cross *dating a celebrity* off of our list on this cruise."

"Well, if there's only one, we'll have to take turns," I said. I didn't mind sharing Brake with Frankie. Not if it meant crossing something off our lifesaving Never-Got-To-Do List.

"I don't think *I'll* ever date again," she said softly, turning to face her laptop screen. "He's all yours."

When we received confirmation that our cruises were booked, and we would share a cabin and a hotel room, we celebrated some more.

We went shopping for cruise clothes. Neither of us had bought new clothes in a few years. "We need to treat ourselves," I said, grateful that our spending spree happened to coincide with end of summer sales. We bought white capris and blouses, and searched for matching blue bathing suits, which Frankie tried on to make sure it fit. I, on the other hand, was not about to try on anything that others might have tried on. And I *certainly* wasn't going to strip down in a flimsy little booth situated right in the middle of a *department store!* Changing rooms were akin to public bathrooms in *my* world, and I wasn't partaking in any of that. I simply bought the largest size of everything and held it up to me in front of the mirror. If it looked like the right size and looked like it would fit, I bought it. I would try it on at home and return it if need be.

Jetta was thrilled about my pending adventure. "When is your flight?" she asked during an early morning call. "I can drive you to the airport so that you don't have to pay to have your car parked there for two weeks."

"They haven't told us when our flights are," I said. "It says all inclusive, so they will probably mail us our plane tickets to get to the ship."

"No, Mom," Jetta said. "All inclusive on a cruise ship doesn't include your transportation to the port of departure. You have to get yourself there."

"I know what I read, Jetta," I told her, annoyed that she had inherited that know-it-all streak from her father. "It said *all inclusive!* If it had required any extra payments on my part, it would have specified."

"Mom, read it again," she said, frustration oozing from every word. "I'm *sure* you'll find on there that it doesn't include transportation to departure point. Trust me, Mom, I've been on a cruise before."

"I'll just call them and find out," I said.

"Well, you better hurry," she said. "If the cruise departs on September first, and you still need to book a flight, you may not be able to get one on this short notice. That's only a week-and-a-half away! Plus, you'll probably have to stay in Los Angeles overnight to make sure you get to the port on time on the day of departure."

I hated that what she was saying was beginning to

make sense to my cruise-virgin ears.

I hung up and called the number on the cruise advertisement, and sure enough, she was correct. I did the math to see how much money we had left. We'd spent the TV show money on our spending spree, and the all-inclusive cruise had cost us $9500.

I called a travel agent, knowing they could somehow magically fix things like this, and was shocked at the price of her fix. "Five thousand dollars?" I shrieked into the phone. *"For two plane seats to Los Angeles? I could hire someone to carry me there on their back for that!"*

"On this short notice," she said flatly. "And to even get them on the day you want, you're looking at first class and that is *short notice first class*. I cannot get it lower than $2500 per person."

"Okay, do it," I said, pulling my credit card out of my purse. "I'm sorry."

"Sorry?" she said. "You won't be getting it?"

"No, I just said sorry to my credit card," I said. "That's how I'll be paying."

I was sure I could hear her smile. "We'll be emailing you the e-tickets."

"The e-tickets?" What the heck is an e-ticket?

"You just have to put the code in at the airport," she said.

"Okay," I agreed, giving her my email address. Jetta would help me figure it out if I couldn't.

As soon as we hung up, I grabbed my notebook and worked out the minimum credit card payment based on my purchase. My credit card had been taking a beating since I quit my last job and with this adventure, including the freshly booked hotel room in Los Angeles, my minimum payment would be $300! That would have to be a worry for another day. I was sure that after a good relaxing vacation, my brain would produce a solution for the money dilemma. Who knows, I could become a grave flipper since I'd done so well on my first transaction! It wasn't exactly the retirement plan I'd envisioned, but it likely wouldn't involve having to get up early.

We were on our way to the airport when I realized that grave flipping carried too much baggage for me.

"I'm so glad that you'll finally get to take a vacation, Mom," Jetta said as she weaved through traffic to get us to the airport on time. "I'm surprised you could get rid of that plot so easily and for the price you were asking!"

"It's easy when soulmates are involved," I said and flashed a smile at Frankie who was all smiles in the back seat.

"Oh?" Jetta asked.

"Yeah, turns out the woman I sold it to was buying it for her mother so she could be buried beside her soulmate," I said. "If I'd been daring, I probably could've sold it to her for twice that."

"*What?*" Jetta asked. "Who did you sell it to, Mom? Was it a woman named Gloria by any chance?"

"I don't know, you know I'm not good with names," I said. "I don't remember what her name was. She was a woman in her thirties who was overdressed with fiery red hair. That's all I remember. Her mother just wanted to be buried beside her soulmate. The man on the other side of the empty plot."

"*Mom!*" Jetta shrieked and slammed on the brakes at an intersection. "You sold it to *Mrs. Ross's daughter, Gloria!*"

"You don't know that!" I said.

"Yes, Mom, I do," Jetta said. "You've described her perfectly. And she's the *only* one that would be willing to pay that much money for that spot!"

"Well, her mother wants to be buried next to her soul mate," I said. "Who cares? I already told you *I* didn't want to be buried there. At least it'll give the guy on the other side his soulmate to spend eternity with."

"Mom, I don't know how to say this," Jetta said slowly with clenched teeth, tightening her grip on the steering wheel. "And I never *wanted* to tell you this," she said. Her nostrils flared, and for a moment I thought she'd forgotten what she was going to say. "I don't think you're gonna want to hear this, Mom, . . . but the person on the other side of that grave is Gloria's *grandmother . . . Dad* is Mrs. Ross's soulmate!"

"*What?*" I asked in shock. "I don't understand what you're saying!"

"Mom, Mrs. Ross and Dad were . . . having an affair," Jetta said, gripping the steering wheel so hard her knuckles were white. "You just sold *your* burial spot to the woman that was having an affair with *your* husband! I hadn't wanted to tell you because you always thought Dad was *so* perfect, but he was seeing *her* while you were in the hospital when I was nine. It was right before you and Dad broke up. I didn't want to tell you about her because I knew you'd be mad. And you kept saying how great Dad was, so I didn't want to upset you, but it's time you found out. *Daddy was a cheater!*"

No wonder Jetta had been so high strung as a child. My heart broke for all the emotions she'd had to keep buried to protect my feelings. I'd *known* Fred had cheated, but up until now, I hadn't even known the names of the women he'd been with.

"It's *okay*, honey," I said, masking my renewed anger at this fresh revelation. "I'm so sorry you had to deal with that all these years, Jetta. I *knew* your father was cheating on me, that's why we broke up. I had no idea of any woman specifically, but I knew he was a cheater. I didn't want you to hate your father, so that's why I never told you anything bad about him. You had a right to a good relationship with your father, even if I didn't have a good relationship with him. I had no idea you were carrying this around."

"It's part of why I hated him so much," she said. "I can't bear the thought of that *awful ugly woman* lying next to Daddy for eternity!"

"I know," I said. "Now I understand why you bought that plot for me. I love you so much for what you tried to do."

We were both silent for a moment while I tried to find the right words to say.

"Honey, look at it this way," I said, scrambling for words that would make us both feel better. "If the highlight of that woman's life is being dead so she can finally be with your father, then let her have that. Who cares? I would say, in the long run, I came out the winner. I'm pursuing *life*, and she's still chasing a *dead guy* who she couldn't fully get during his lifetime! The only reason she thinks she can have him now is because he's unable to get away from her!"

Jetta smiled despite herself, and her grip on the steering wheel relaxed a little. She was probably more upset about *me* finding out about Fred and Mrs. Ross than she was about Mrs. Ross herself.

I looked back at Frankie to see how she was handling all this talk about death and graves. Not the ideal way to start a vacation. But I was relieved to see her stifling a smile over my view of the situation.

"I can never forgive him or her," Jetta said. "I'm going to find a way to get that grave back."

"Oh, honey, don't worry about it," I said. "If it

means that much to you, *I* will get it back from her when I get home, okay?"

"How?" she asked. "She won't part with that now!"

"Oh, Jetta, Jetta, Jetta," I said, shaking my head for emphasis. "It's like you don't even know me! I'll not only get the grave back, but I'll get her to *give it back to me for free!*"

She was silent, but I knew she could believe me. I could move mountains when I wanted to. A hole in the ground should be no problem! And I was determined to set off on my new adventure with a clear mind. If I could ignore a looming credit card bill, I sure as heck could ignore a delusional woman pursuing a dead guy! I was not going to let *anything* ruin the biggest adventure of my life!

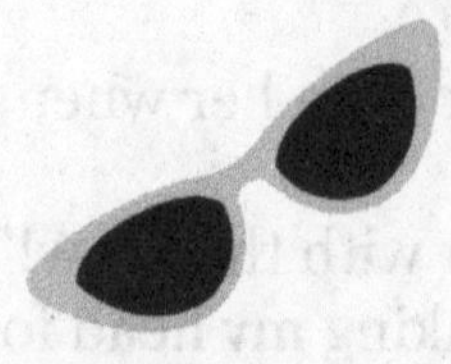

Chapter 13: Brake Caldwell

After being seated in oversized comfy seats and being told we were not being charged for our excessive baggage of cruise clothes, I decided I would never fly coach again! My fear of heights meant that Frankie got to sit by the window, and we were both happy.

The in-flight meal consisted of grilled chicken, mashed potatoes, and soggy looking peas that was served on real plates with real stainless-steel silverware.

"I feel like a queen," Frankie whispered.

"Me too," I said. "And we deserve this. Just think, by this time tomorrow afternoon we'll be on a ship with *Brake Caldwell!* You know what that means!"

"What?" She looked at me curiously.

"That he can't get away from us unless he jumps in the ocean!" I said.

We both laughed. I felt like a teenager again, and I could tell that Frankie did too. She was not the same person I'd rescued from her hovel six weeks ago.

"Would you ladies like dessert?" the lovely young stewardess asked.

"Just coffee for me," Frankie said.

"I'll have dessert and coffee," I said, eyeing the huge chunk of cake on her tray.

Frankie nudged me in the side with her elbow. "We'll be meeting *Brake Caldwell*," she whispered.

"You know what, just coffee for me too," I said to

the stewardess. I eyed that gorgeous chunk of chocolate cake as she returned it to her tray.

I jealously watched the people across the aisle who gobbled up the cake without a care about their waistlines or Brake Caldwell.

"You know, I never thought I'd get to go anywhere," Frankie said. "Much less first class! I don't know how I can ever repay you!"

"I don't know how I can ever repay *myself!*" I said, thinking of my poor credit card.

We got high-end comfy headphones to listen to a movie with, but we were both so excited about our vacation that we just talked nonstop instead.

"I wonder if he's single," I said.

"Who cares?" Frankie answered. "As long as we get to meet *Brake Caldwell!*"

When we arrived in Los Angeles, I was shocked when I saw a man in a suit holding up a sign with our names on it.

"What on earth?" I asked Frankie, stopping right in the midst of the disembarking passengers who had to funnel around either side of us.

"Remember? The woman in the airport said it was one of the perks of first class! She said that we'd have a car to drive us to the hotel," she said.

"I didn't hear her say that," I said. "I was too busy fantasizing about the free extra luggage I could bring back with souvenirs."

"Well, she said part of our first-class airline deal included a car to transport us from the airport to the hotel," Frankie said, walking straight for the well-dressed stranger with the sign.

"Frankie, you know what this means?" I hurried and grabbed her arm so I could whisper in her ear. *"We're getting a limo ride!"*

"Oh my gosh, it's on our list!" she said in hushed excitement. "We're going to ride in a limo!"

"Frances Krane and Philadelphia Powers?" the driver asked.

"Yes, sir!" I said enthusiastically.

"Right this way," he said, and we followed him from the airport to our waiting limo that turned out to be an SUV.

"That's not a limousine," Frankie said in shock.

"No Ma'am," the driver said, deftly opening the back door for us. "It is a Cadillac Escalade."

"It still counts," I whispered to Frankie as I practically had to push her into the car.

"No, it does *not* count," Frankie whispered. For some reason she looked like the excitement had been drained out of her. It wasn't like we'd *expected* a vehicle in the first place! I didn't understand how she could be so picky.

"It's better than a cab," I told her. "And it's the service that counts. We're receiving limo treatment, so it counts!"

"No, it looks more like a hearse!" she said.

"What? It does not!" I argued. I was irritated that she could be so unappreciative. "Why can't you just enjoy it? We got picked up by a *chauffeur!* And we are in *a Cadillac!"*

"Because," she said evenly, "the last time I saw a car like this, it was to go to a funeral." It was clear that Edgar's death wasn't something she could get over in a mere two years, but it wasn't like we could just get out of a moving car.

I should've known talking about a grave on the way to the airport was a bad idea. Then to get off and be met with a vehicle that gave Frankie flashbacks must have been traumatic for her. I realized that she hadn't processed even the fact that her husband had died. She hadn't arranged his funeral, packed up his things, or done anything that in any way acknowledged he'd even died. She'd never actually properly grieved his death and was holding on to it, as if the grief was the only part of him that was now tangible. I realized that in that instant, as I was feeling like a princess, she was feeling like a widow.

"Tomorrow we'll be on the cruise," I assured her, patting her hand. "And we'll see Brake Caldwell."

"Okay," she said flatly, turning away and staring out the window. Probably so I couldn't see her cry, but I wasn't stupid, and I'd known her forever. "But we're taking a taxi to the port!"

"Of course!" I agreed.

We had a quick dinner in the hotel restaurant, and then I spent the evening trying to renew Frankie's excitement for the cruise. But she was more reserved than she'd been since we booked this adventure. I tried to spark a conversation, but she was sullen.

"I'm sleepy, and we should probably get some rest," she said quietly.

"It's only eight o'clock!"

"The boat begins boarding at eleven in the morning," she said. "By the time we get up and shower and eat, that time will go by fast."

"Okay," I said. So, we put the lights out, and she crawled into her bed in Edgar's pajamas and faced the wall. I decided to give her the privacy to cry. "Well, I'm going to go down and check out the gift shop before it closes," I said. "I'll be back in about a half hour."

I took my purse and left the room. It would give her time to let out her emotions without feeling embarrassed, and I would buy her a little surprise from the gift shop to help her feel better afterwards.

As soon as I walked into the gift shop, Brake Caldwell's face drew me in like a magnet. A whole shelf of books facing the door had his face on the cover. I had no idea he'd written a book. I knew he hadn't acted in years, but I had no idea he *could* do anything other than act. I apparently liked my men one-dimensional. I investigated further and purchased two copies of Brake Caldwell's *Keto Hollywood Secrets*. It had to be a good book. I had no idea what kind of secret keto was, but I loved a good mystery. It sounded familiar so I knew I must've heard it somewhere before.

I took my purchases to the lounge area and decided to sit and read for a little while to give Frankie ample time to cool down. I'd just opened the cover of the book when I vaguely noticed a man enter the lounge and sit in an armchair across from me.

"Oh, I see you picked up a great book!" he said.

"Yes," I said, not even looking up. Nothing was going to take my attention away from Brake Caldwell!

"Would you like it autographed?" he asked.

That's an odd question, I thought and looked up into the familiar face of *Brake Caldwell!*

Chapter 14: Fan Girls

I stared into Brake Caldwell's face, wanted to say something—anything—but my mind was *completely* blank.

"Sorry to interrupt your reading," he said with a little chuckle. He was just as handsome as he used to be, but he looked at least ten years older than his photo on the book cover.

"No, no, that's quite alright," I said. "Trust me!"

He chuckled some more. "Seriously, not to sound full of myself, but I *will* autograph it for you if you like."

"Hootin' banana crackers! Of course!" I said, handing it over calmly in an outwardly mature way, while my mind was screaming, *Brake Caldwell is actually having a conversation with me!* I grabbed the second book out of the bag. "And please sign this one for my friend, Frankie."

He took the second book, opened it, and deftly signed the book for Frankie with a black felt-tipped pen he obviously carried for this purpose. I didn't know many—or any—men that walked around prepared with a black felt-tipped pen!

"And what's *your* name?" he asked as he embarked on a second autograph.

"Del," I said.

"Del? Short for Adele?" he asked. *He was interested in my name!*

"No, short for Philadelphia," I said.

"Wow, that's an impressive name," he said with a surprised grin. "Your parents were quite unique."

"Yeah, that's what my first-grade teacher said," I told him. "I was the only kid that had to write my name on both sides of the paper because it was so long, and my handwriting was so messy."

He laughed. "You are hilarious," he said with a grin.

"Yeah, I've been told that," I admitted. *We're having a real conversation!* "So, are you staying in this hotel?"

"Don't look so surprised," he said. "Washed up movie stars need to sleep somewhere too."

"You're hilarious, too," I said. "But I'd hardly call you washed up. Clearly, you've been busy."

"I haven't acted for quite a while," he said. "I wrote a few mystery novels, but they were kind of a flop. I wrote this keto book, and it seemed to take off, go figure. Do you do keto?"

"I'm just starting," I said, having absolutely no clue what keto even was. A cult? A religion? "Do you?"

He laughed. "Yes, that's why I wrote the book; it totally changed my life."

"Duh, of course!" I said, shaking my head as though I'd somehow absent-mindedly forgotten that I was holding his keto book, while simultaneously feeling my face catch on fire in embarrassment. "Maybe it would be good for my friend too."

"It's good for everyone probably," he said. "I don't like to say that it's *definitely* good for *everyone* because, you know, I'm not a doctor or anything, and I don't want to get sued for giving medical advice. But this book is just about how it worked for *me*, and how it changed my life."

I still had no idea what keto was. Was it an exercise regimen? A vitamin? An alcoholic drink? I had no clue. I didn't want to look stupid, so I had to keep my statements vague.

"I'm probably not going to be as good at it as you are," I said. "Because I'm so out of shape. Are you supposed to do it every day? Or like, once a week?"

He laughed. "It's all in the book."

Okay, clearly it wasn't something I could *do*. It must be something one could *experience*. It was probably a mindset, like believing in yourself or something. I would definitely have to read the book and find out!

"Well, it was really nice meeting you, Philadelphia," he said. "I love your name, by the way—but I don't like leaving Uncle Oscar alone for too long, and tomorrow is going to be a really long day for me, so I best get some rest."

"Nice meeting you, too!" I said. "And thank you!"

I hurried back up to the room and opened the door quietly in case Frankie had actually gone to sleep. But she was in the bathroom. I heard her blow her nose, wash her hands and then come out.

"Where did you go?" she asked.

"Well, I got you something," I said and handed over her copy of Brake's book.

"Oh my gosh! Where did you get this?" she said. "I had no *idea* he wrote a book!"

"Yeah, I didn't either," I said. "But open it! *Open it!*"

She opened the cover slowly. "*What?* How did you do this? Where did you get this?"

"I just ran into him down in the lobby," I said. "*And he said he loved my name!*"

"No way!" she said.

"Yes way!" I said. "And he's staying in this very hotel!"

"Why didn't you come get me?" she demanded.

"You said you were going to sleep," I reminded her.

"Okay, that's *it!*" she said. "From now on, I'm not letting you out of my sight, because every time I do, you end up getting all chummy with a celebrity, and I miss out!"

I opened my book and read what he'd written. *Enjoy your keto journey, Philadelphia! Love, Brake Caldwell.* "What does yours say?"

"Mine says, 'to Frankie, enjoy your keto journey, love Brake Caldwell,'" she said.

"Mine too," I said. "He obviously writes that to everyone. I think he considers his book a journey." I laughed.

"No, it's the cruise!" she said.

"What are you talking about?" I asked.

"The cruise is called a Keto Cruise. Look!" She reached over, grabbed her purse off her nightstand and fished out the cruise ticket. "See? The name of the cruise is Keto Cruise."

"Oh, that's weird," I said. "So, maybe his health fix was a cruise."

"Huh?" she asked.

"He said keto changed his life," I said. "So, I guess this cruise should be good for *us* too!"

"So, you told him we're going on the cruise too?" she asked.

"No, but probably everyone staying in this hotel is going on the cruise," I said.

"That's unlikely," she said.

"Well, how would *he* know we're going on the Keto Cruise then?" I asked.

"I don't know," she admitted. "You *must've* said it."

"I'm telling you, I didn't," I said. "Remember when you didn't believe me about meeting Darwin Beckett?"

She shrugged. "Well, whatever keto means, we'll probably find out on the cruise."

"Or we *could* just read his book," I said logically.

But it was late and instead of reading it, we alternated between staring at his picture on the front cover and running our fingers over his *authentic* autograph.

When we finally decided we had to get some sleep so we didn't miss our boat in the morning, we turned off the light, but I couldn't turn off my thoughts.

"Goodnight, Frankie," I said.

"Goodnight, Del," she replied.

"I'm proud of you," I said.

"What? Why?" she asked rolling over to face me. "What brought that on?"

"Well, I just admire how strong you are," I said. "You've been through a lot and you're still willing to go on adventures with me."

"Always," she said. "It feels good to start living again."

After she was snoring, which was an annoying habit I was willing to tolerate for our friendship, I lay there thinking. I tried not to think of the mounting debt but had a momentary doubt about the wisdom in spending every last cent—*and beyond*—just to take a cruise. And those hardcover books weren't cheap either. At least the autograph was free—and yet priceless!

A lightbulb went off in my head. I wondered how much an autographed copy of a Brake Caldwell book would be worth. Not that I could see myself ever being able to part with it, but it was a nice thing to keep in the back of my mind just in case.

I decided not to damage my copy at all because I had a feeling that it *might* just have to go towards paying off my credit card when I got home. Before I went to sleep, I carefully slipped my book back into the little bag it had come in and placed it gently on my nightstand. This keto book had the potential to change *my* life financially, at least a little. I hoped.

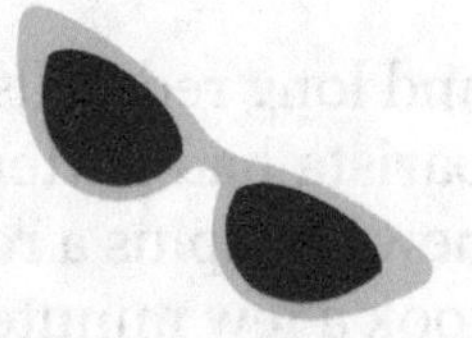

Chapter 15: The Keto Cruise

Full of excitement, we arrived at the port of San Pedro with two hours to spare. I, for one, was *definitely not* going to miss *this* boat!

As soon as we got out of the cab, a porter took our luggage, tagged with our names and cabin number, and told us they would automatically be delivered to our room later in the afternoon. A lady in a uniform pointed to a waiting area. "You'll hear an announcement when it is time for you to board."

"You mean, we can't board early?" I asked in surprise.

"No," she said, looking at my boarding pass. "You can board at the time on your boarding pass, which says eleven o'clock."

So, Frankie and I and our bulky carry-on bags and purses maneuvered to some curvy blue seats to sit and wait. "I told you we didn't need to leave this early," Frankie mumbled as we sat down, still a bit peeved that I'd rushed her through her breakfast which caused her to complain several times about indigestion. "If I'd had time to drink my coffee, I wouldn't be so miserable right now."

"Oh, for Pete's sake," I said, my own lack of caffeine kicking in. "You can get coffee right over there, and it's better to be early than it is to be late! And get me one, too." She got up in a huff and went over to the coffee counter. She had to wait for a rich-looking woman in heavy makeup and long red nails to complain quite loudly about how the barista had gotten her coffee wrong, and she demanded a new one, plus a refund for making her late for boarding. It took a few minutes for her to get appeased enough to walk away and click by me in loud heels.

I turned to see how *she* would react to being told she couldn't board yet. I watched her march right past the port staff that had made *me* wait—and not one of them made an effort to stop the mad rich woman. Of course, that woman hadn't had her morning coffee either, so they probably didn't dare.

While I sat and wondered how long Frankie would be annoyed at my early morning rush, I watched a glamorous couple glide by. They looked like movie stars, but if they *had* been, I would've recognized them. I turned to see how *they* would react when they got turned away for being too early. To my shock, the girl in the uniform smiled and waved them on toward the ship.

"Oh no she *didn't!*" I shot out of my seat like a woman possessed. "How come everyone else can board but my friend and me? Is it just because *we're* not rich Hollywood stars?"

The poor girl looked shocked. "Ma'am, we board in groups to prevent congestion," she said. "That's why each group is assigned different boarding times. It ensures that everyone has a pleasant experience."

My jaw dropped and my face got hot in humiliation.

"Oh, so *my* group boards at eleven," I said, taking my tone down a notch, suddenly trying to sound reasonable. As if I hadn't just accused her of conspiring against middle-class mortals like me.

"Yes," she said with a patient smile. "And that group boards at nine."

"Okay, just making sure it wasn't because of my

age," I muttered, scrambling to pretend I had a shred of dignity left.

"Oh no!" she said cheerfully. "We have plenty of senior citizens!"

She called me a *senior citizen!* And there went my shred! I slinked back to my seat, mortified, as Frankie returned with our coffees.

"Man, I can't leave you alone for one second!" Frankie said as she chuckled. It wasn't a good-natured chuckle; it was the kind that said *serves you right!*

At last, we were walking down the gangplank that would allow us to check off the most exciting thing on our list! The ship loomed above us like a gleaming palace, and we could hardly contain our excitement. Frankie squeezed my arm as we stepped on board, whispering, "I can't believe *we're really doing this*, Del!" I knew exactly what she was feeling. This was the start of something magical!

"First on the agenda is finding Brake!" I said. I was dismayed that he wasn't in the main entry area to greet guests. *What exactly does hosting a cruise even mean?*

A guy in a white cruise shirt and white shorts handed us a paper. "This is our daily newsletter," the guy said. He was in his forties and looked like he'd started out as a paperboy, and no one had ever told him he could have another job. His knee-length shorts added to the image. I smiled and Frankie looked at me quizzically. "Have a wonderful cruise!" he said as he pulled out another paper to hand to the couple behind us.

"Oh, look!" Frankie pointed out. Right near the top of the newsletter was a picture of Brake. "It says he'll be greeting guests at the Sail Away Party on the Lido Deck at four!"

"Okay then!" I said, filled with hope. "Let's find our room and get rid of these carry-ons."

After thirty minutes of getting lost—twice—a nice cabin steward led us to our cabin.

"Aw, we have an interior room," Frankie said. "I hoped we'd get a room with a window so we could get a look at the ocean."

"Well, we aren't going to be spending much time in our room," I said. I didn't want to tell her I'd saved a ton of money just by selecting an interior room. I had no desire to spend the extra money on a window. Not when we were *surrounded* by ocean and could look at it from anywhere on the ship! "Why stare at the ocean when you can do that from any beach on land? Besides, we came to stare at *Brake,* not the ocean."

"Right!" she said. "Oh, let's take our books, so he knows we're really reading them."

I hadn't even begun reading mine, but she was right. Still, I didn't want to drag my book around in the humid air and have it ruin the resale value, in case I did need to sell it. "I think it's okay if just one of us takes the book," I said. "You should bring yours."

So, with her *Keto Hollywood Secrets* tucked under her arm, she followed me on a journey to find the Lido deck. It was still hours away from the party time, but I figured Brake might show up early. Maybe we could get a chance to have a conversation with him before it got crowded. *I hoped.*

The Lido deck was a huge pool area, surrounded by plenty of blue loungers, and lined on the perimeter with massive eating areas and snack bars. There was already a small crowd when we got there. Not so crowded that there weren't plenty of loungers available for us to choose from but crowded enough that we wouldn't be easily noticeable to Brake.

"Well, it's going to be hours before he gets here, and

I'm kind of hungry," I admitted. "Let's check out the food!"

We went over to the snack bar and eyed the various signs and snacks in glass cages. "Wow, all of this looks delicious!" Frankie said.

Everything looked foreign and delicious, but I had no clue what anything was. The guy behind the counter must've noticed our dilemma. "Would you like a snack?" he asked. "They are free."

"Yes," I said and wondered if he'd stressed the word free because we looked more like desperate housewives than two fun-loving women on a quest for adventure. "But I have no idea what to get."

"Keto friendly?" he asked. *That was a weird question.* Then it hit me. Frankie was clutching Brake's keto book.

"Oh, yes," I said. "We're *very* keto friendly!"

"Okay," he said and pointed at the big round chocolate balls. "These are Almond Butter Fat Bombs."

"What's in them?" I asked.

"Coconut oil, almond butter, and xylitol, and a touch of salt," he said. I had no idea what xylitol was, but it *sounded* like alcohol.

"Well, don't want to get tipsy," I said. "But I guess it couldn't hurt to try one."

He smiled and placed one on a napkin with a pair of tongs. "I'll try one too," Frankie said. She took a bite. "Oh . . . my . . . gosh! *This* is my new favorite food! I'll worry about my diet later!"

We had lunch at a huge buffet. "Look!" Frankie pointed to a big sign over a section of the offerings that said in big letters, *Keto Friendly*. I pushed her into that line. In case, unbeknownst to us, Brake happened to be looking, I wanted it to be very clear to everyone within viewing distance that Frankie and I were *definitely* keto friendly! All while pushing aside the growing worry that keto seemed to be something extreme, requiring segregated eating sections. *If people had to be segregated based on their friendliness to this group of people, I was not going to be one that would appear hostile! I didn't come on this cruise to make enemies!*

Finally, it was time for the Sail Away party and neither Frankie nor I knew what to expect, so we stood as close to the stage area as we could.

"I hope he recognizes me from last night," I said. "Hold your book higher so he can see it."

"Since you guys hit it off so well, maybe he'll have dinner with us," she said.

"I can ask," I said, as if I actually had the power to influence him. "He *was* very friendly last night."

Screaming on the other side of the pool caught our attention, and it was then that I realized that there were *two* stages! The one where we were, and a raised one on the other side that was where a throng of middle-aged women jostled for positioning to be closer to Brake.

"Marry me!" one of them screamed as if *both* he and she were young and beautiful. Well, *he* was, but I could not say the same for her. She looked like she was someone's grandmother, and I was embarrassed for her. I mean, I would've *thought* the same thing, but I had way too much self-awareness to *shout it at the top of my lungs!*

"Come on," I said to Frankie. We pushed our way through the rapidly growing crowd until we were as close as we could get to Brake, which was not close at all.

He introduced himself and waved at the crowd. I wasn't exactly paying attention to *what* he was saying, I was just watching him speak and admiring how he was still gorgeous after all these years. I'd been so star-struck the night before that my first encounter with him had been a blur of shock and amazement and a racing heart over the fact that he'd *spoken* to me. I'd been so jarred by the difference in his image on the book cover to how he looked in real life, that he had appeared older and grayer than he did just now. *Could he have dyed his hair overnight?* I wondered.

"We have to get closer," I said to Frankie and continued pushing my way through the crowd, dragging her along behind me. I received a lot of foul looks as I tried to get even closer. Finally, I managed to get a prime position that—if the big blonde woman in front of me moved the right way—he could see me. I waved every time his eyes were vaguely in my direction, but either he didn't recognize me, or he just didn't see me—leaving me totally embarrassed and wondering what the people on either side of me were thinking. Probably the same thing I had been thinking about the woman that yelled at him to marry her!

I kept running my hand through my hair to try to catch his eye. But nope, nothing I did caught his attention. Then he handed the microphone to some other guy in a blue shirt who introduced himself as our cruise director. Music played, and the guy waved his arms in the air while directing the passengers to follow his movements. Brake disappeared.

"Where did he go?" I asked Frankie.

"I have no clue," she said.

"There!" I said, pointing as he was weaving his way through an exit *and walking away!* "Hurry!" We pushed through the crowd as fast as we could, but he made it into the elevator just before we reached him.

"Brake!" I yelled, but only the man getting into the elevator behind him glanced at me, squinting through his small circular glasses. He rushed into the elevator and the door closed before we reached it.

I jabbed at the button to the adjacent elevator, but it flashed red.

"You have to tap your SeaPass," Frankie pointed out at the icon of the card above a scanner. I frantically dug through my bag and tapped the pass. The rectangular LED screen above the elevator button flashed a big red *declined* message.

"Oh, look," Frankie pointed to the other sign above the elevators that said *VIP Elevators*.

So, while other passengers, seemingly *all* of them danced to the loud music, or waved to the port as we left shore, Frankie and I waited beside the VIP elevators until a crew member came along and wheeled a food cart into one.

I grabbed Frankie and we stepped inside, holding our heads high as if we belonged in that elevator. I noticed that there were three extra floors on this elevator panel that were not on the elevator we'd come down on. I had no idea which floor Brake would be on. I quickly debated whether this food cart was destined for *his* room and whether we should get off with the waiter or try to be more subtle and get off at another floor. But I waited too long, and it would've looked ridiculous for me to press another button by the time I realized I probably should have.

The waiter looked at me and asked, "How are you ladies enjoying your cruise?"

"Oh, it is simply delightful!" I said with a British accent that came out of nowhere.

"Yes, simply mah-velous!" Frankie chimed in, lifting her chin in the air like royalty.

"Oh, Francesca," I said. "We simply *must* try the keto pool!"

"Oh, yes, Philadelphia," she replied. "But first I must change into my keto swimsuit!"

"Of course, Dah-ling," I said. "And I'll grab my keto purse!"

We all got off at the Vista Deck. The waiter was polite and nodded with a tight smile and a raised eyebrow but didn't say anything as he got off the elevator. I pulled Frankie down the hall in the opposite direction with confident strides as if we had a definite destination. I didn't want it to look to the waiter like we didn't even have a room to go to. As soon as we turned the corner, I wheeled around and peeked, waiting to see who opened the door for the food, hoping it would be Brake. Much to my disappointment, it was that beautiful couple that had boarded at nine.

"Well, that was anticlimactic!" I said and we waited until the waiter had disappeared before heading back to the elevator. I jabbed at the button and was surprised to see that the SeaPass display flashed red. "What a pain," I said. "Now what do we do?"

"There has to be stairs around here," Frankie said. "Let's look at the end of the hall."

It was like the thinking part of my brain got turned off when I was excited. We trudged down flight after flight of stairs, with increasing groans at every level, until we got to a floor with a regular elevator.

Later that night as we settled down for our first night's sleep on the ocean, my achy knee helped me realize two things. One: I wasn't as young as I thought I was or wanted to be. Two: "We need to find out his room number!"

"Good night, Del!" Frankie said and rolled over.

Chapter 16: A VIP Fight

"What do you mean, you can't tell me what cabin he's in?" I demanded of the stocky forty-something woman that looked like she could take me on if it came to a physical altercation.

"I'm sorry, we can't give out personal information about our guests," she said.

"But your sign says Guest Services!" I reminded her. "And he's my friend!"

"Well then, why don't you just ask him yourself?" she asked. I was fuming. Guest Services was not helping me at all.

"He told me, but I forgot," I lied. Even I was aware that I'm a pretty poor liar.

"Look, ma'am," she said firmly. "I am *not* going to give you Brake Caldwell's cabin number!" I knew the conversation was over by her tone.

"Come on, Del," Frankie said as she pulled me away from the Guest Services desk. "Let's just go relax by the pool for a while."

As we walked away, I heard the Guest Services woman tell her coworker. "That was the *fifth* one today!" Her coworker laughed, while I slinked away.

I grudgingly allowed Del to pull me towards the Lido deck. "Who knows," she said, "maybe he'll come for a swim sometime."

"We have to upgrade!" I said as soon as I sat down.

"Who knows what kind of stuff the VIP people have up there? They could even have their *own* pool that we can't even get to, for all I know."

"I don't think so," she said slowly, but it was clear she didn't know. How could she? This was a first cruise for both of us!

"We have to do something," I said. "For the past two days, I think we've walked through every square inch of this ship! I swear I'm losing weight! My shorts are getting loose on me, look!" I put my hand beneath the waistband of my shorts and showed her the gap between the material and my abdomen.

"Well, walking is good for us," she said. "I think my clothes are getting looser too!"

"I'm either going to upgrade us or demand my money back," I told her. "We paid for a cruise to *see* Brake Caldwell. They used his face to make us buy this cruise, and we haven't seen him since his two-minute appearance yesterday!"

Frankie stretched out in the lounger and pulled Brake's book out of her beach bag. "I'm going to read," she said. "So that if we ever *do* meet him, at least I can talk to him about his book."

"Frankie!" *I could not believe her blasé attitude!* "We don't have *time* to read at a time like this! In two days, we'll be in Hawaii. Do you know how big Hawaii is? Once we're on land, we will probably not even see him at all. Then we only have four days back. I don't want to meet him on the last day and then not have any time to spend with him! The clock is ticking, and I want to meet him ASAP!"

"Del, just for *once* could you not be over dramatic?" she said, opening the book. "You're ruining *this* never-got-to-do by *another* never-got-to-do. We don't have to go on a cruise *and* date a celebrity all in one go! Why don't we just relax and enjoy this? That's what cruises are for!"

"But, Frankie, when you have a cruise *and* a celebrity all at the same time, why not just cross *both* things off at once?" My words fell on deaf ears. "Besides, it's *Brake Caldwell!*"

"Look, Del, this may be the only cruise I ever get to go on," she said, staring at me with an expression that looked so mature, I felt like a teenager arguing with *my mother* again! It was clear she had no real interest in Brake Caldwell. While I was relieved to have eliminated *one* member of my competition, I was scared because *I'd lost her!* She'd turned into some middle-aged woman mid-cruise, and now I was on my own to pursue my dream date with Brake Caldwell. I knew I'd never have another chance where he and I would be in such close proximity. I wasn't going to waste this opportunity!

"Suit yourself," I said. "But you know that you're wasting *your* never-got-to-do cruise by reading when you can just read at home!"

"Del, I just want to relax and enjoy this vacation," she said. "You do what you want, but I'll be here until dinnertime."

"Fine!" I muttered as I turned and walked away. "If I *do* manage to meet Brake and wrangle a date with him, *you're* not invited!"

I marched back down to the Guest Services desk and was sure I saw the woman roll her eyes as she saw me approach.

"Hi," I said as sweetly as I could manage. "How do I upgrade my cabin to VIP?"

She looked relieved. "Oh, I can help you with that," she said and went to work on her computer. "We do have one available on Sky Deck. The passenger was a no show. It will be $5000 to upgrade."

"Can you take a credit card?" I asked, ready to sacrifice my other credit card I'd paid off a year ago—and had vowed never to touch again except in an extreme emergency. *This* was an extreme emergency.

"Everything on board is charged to your account with your SeaPass," she said. "Our steward will show you to your new room, and I will have to switch your card. We can have a butler pack your things for you and deliver them to your new room."

"A butler?" I could see why the upgrade was so expensive. When they labeled something VIP, they weren't messing around. "There are two of us, so I better pack." I said, deciding to make it a surprise for Frankie.

As soon as I'd packed up our belongings, a steward took me up in the VIP elevator to the Sky Deck and opened a door to the most beautiful, luxurious room. It was more like a spacious hotel room, complete with a separate seating area and little table, as well as a sliding door and a balcony that looked out on the ocean. *Frankie is gonna love this!*

"You can press this button on the phone for the butler," the steward pointed out. "He will bring you anything you need."

I was bursting with excitement when I went searching for Frankie to give her the new SeaPass. She was no longer by the pool. I checked the snack bars and the restaurants, but no Frankie. A surge of jealousy shot through me as I thought perhaps, she'd managed to find Brake, and she was with him somewhere.

When I finally ran into her in a corridor, we were both fuming.

"Where were you?" I asked suspiciously.

"Why did you lock me out of our room?" she demanded, waving her SeaPass around. "You can be so childish, sometimes, Del! Just because I didn't want to go on your stalking activities, you locked me out of the room?"

"Stop!" I held up my hand. I knew if either one of us said another word, our friendship would not withstand this cruise. "I have a surprise for you."

"Del, I'm tired of surprises!" she exclaimed, and I couldn't understand why she looked so fed up with me. "I've had enough surprises in my life! I just want to relax! Is that too much to ask?"

I snatched her SeaPass out of her hand. "If you really want this, you can have it," I said. "But you're gonna have to pay for it yourself."

I paused and was ashamed at how much joy I got out of her shifting expressions from shock to anger to vengeance.

"Or," I said, pausing for emphasis. "You can have *this SeaPass.*"

She just eyed me silently and stared at the crimson color of the new VIP pass.

"To our new room on the VIP floor," I said. "Come with me!" We both ignored our smoldering anger while she followed me to the Guest Services desk where I turned in her old card. Then I proudly ushered her into the VIP elevator and took her to the Sky Deck and directly to our new room.

"Oh . . . my . . . gosh!" she said, spinning around to take in the luxurious room—from the cream-colored Egyptian cotton duvet covers and plush pink carpeting to a silver plate of chocolates on the nightstand. "Del, I should've known you'd do something over the top like this! You really shouldn't have. This must've cost you a *fortune.*"

She hurried across the room and slid open the balcony door, ushering in the roar of the sea.

I stood with my arms folded, waiting for her to notice how much she'd hurt my feelings. Eventually, her eyes met mine, and the flicker of guilt told me she knew what I was waiting for.

"I'm sorry," she said sheepishly. "I feel like a fool. I just felt like we've been more stressed on this cruise than we ever were before, and I just wanted to relax a little."

I shrugged, trying to brush it off, and gestured toward the plush cream-colored sofa. "I get it," I said. "Now you can relax all you want in comfort!"

Frankie plopped onto the sofa and a smile instantly spread across her face. "Okay, you win," she said. "I can't deny this is luxurious!"

I nodded and tried to ignore the heavy feeling that settled in my chest. It seemed like all of our fun was on me. I was the motivator, the cheerleader, the idea person, and the financial provider. Sometimes I felt like she dragged me down. But I pushed that thought aside for now and plopped down beside her. I was smart enough to know that the biggest thing eating at me right now was the growing debt, and I was beginning to wonder *myself* if it really was worth it.

"By the way," I said as a knock sounded on our door. "We have a butler now."

Frankie looked at me, confused, as I opened it to find a well-dressed man with a perfectly knotted tie and our luggage in tow.

"Your luggage, ma'am," he said smoothly, setting the suitcases neatly inside the room. He handed me a card and gave a slight bow. "I am Jeffrey, your butler. Please don't hesitate to call if you need anything."

"Oh my gosh!" Frankie whispered as the door closed behind him. "We have a butler? Like, a *real* butler?"

"Yes," I said, unable to resist a grin. "And he'll bring us anything we need."

"Anything?" Frankie asked, her eyes wide with possibility.

"Well, within reason," I said, trying to sound practical even though my mind raced with all the potential luxuries we could indulge in.

Frankie stared at the card with a look of awe. "I can't believe we have a butler!"

"This is the life! Flying first class! Getting a VIP cabin!" I said, flopping onto the sofa. "*We* have a butler. This is VIP!"

Frankie smiled, her earlier frustration melting away and taking mine with it. "You know what? Maybe *this* never-got-to-do *was* meant to be done in style!"

Chapter 17: Brake and Uncle Oscar

On the third day of the cruise, I was up early, excited to renew my pursuit of Brake and was surprised to see that Frankie was gone. I knew she had no storage room to go cry in, and it was unlike her to go to breakfast without me. *Maybe she just needs some privacy.* After all, she and I had been practically joined at the hip since she'd moved in. She was probably by the VIP pool now, trying to get a jump on Brake before I was even up.

I called Jeffery as soon as I was dressed. "Can you please tell me what room Brake Caldwell is in?" I asked him.

"Oh, I'm sorry, ma'am," he said. "I cannot violate the privacy of our VIP guests."

"But *I'm* a VIP guest," I reminded him.

"Yes, and likewise, I will not be giving out *your* personal information to other people," he said. Well, I had to appreciate that.

"But you *do* know what room he's in though, right?" I asked.

"Ma'am, is there anything I can help you with that does not involve another passenger's privacy?" he asked.

"All I'm saying is, if I were to give you a note to give to him, seeing as how he's my friend, could you give it to him for me?"

"Yes, I don't see anything wrong with that," he said.

"Would you like me to book dinner reservations for you?"

"Sure," I said. "Is that where *he* eats?"

"Ma'am," he said with an expression very similar to the girl's at the Guest Services desk.

"I know, but I paid to come on this cruise specifically because *he* was hosting it, and I haven't seen a trace of him since his first two-minute greeting on departure day," I explained.

"Haven't you been attending the keto lectures?" he asked. "He is there every afternoon."

"No," I said slowly. "I didn't *know* about them. And I've been too busy running all over this keto ship to bother going to any lectures. What are they about?"

"Um," he looked at me with a wrinkled brow. "Keto, ma'am."

"I know, you said that," I said. "This ship is called keto. His book is called keto. Everything is called keto. I wish someone would explain to me what that word even means!"

He gave me a half-smile. "Keto is a way of eating, ma'am," he said. "It's short for ketogenic diet."

"A diet?" I asked. "I came on a *diet* cruise?"

"More like a way of life," he said. "A high fat, low carbohydrate diet puts your body in a state of ketosis where your body breaks down excess fat into ketone bodies and water."

"Is that why I seem to be losing weight?" I asked in shock.

"If you've been eating from the keto friendly menu, then most likely," he said.

"Oh," I said slowly as it dawned on me that I'd been looking like an idiot by telling everyone *I* was keto friendly. "I had no idea what it meant. I thought it was like a religion or something."

He smiled instinctively. "Just a way of eating that allows your body to recover from years of junk foods and sugar."

"Oh, I am *so* embarrassed," I said.

At that moment, Frankie barged into the room holding up two pair of flip-flops. "Oh, hi, Jeffrey," she said. "Look, Del, I got us some keto flip-flops!"

"No, you didn't," I said with a laugh. I explained to her what keto was and she was equally embarrassed.

"Oh my gosh," she said. "I just spent a half an hour telling the girl in the sandal shop that I was the keto friendliest person I knew!"

"You know the keto lectures are every afternoon at four," Jeffrey said. "It's all on your daily newsletter that gets delivered to your room each morning."

"So, Brake Caldwell should be at those, right?" I asked.

He smiled. "Yes, and also a medical doctor who gives lectures about it."

"Well, I'm going to actually read Brake's book so that I don't look like a complete idiot," Frankie said after Jeffrey left.

"I thought you already were reading it," I said.

"No, I got so annoyed with you yesterday that I couldn't settle my mind enough to read."

"Well, you read, I'm going to go explore the VIP areas to see if I can see Brake," I said and left.

For being a high-profile guest, he was certainly elusive. I explored a VIP gym, deck, lounge and theater and still didn't find him.

Finally, it was getting close to three o'clock, so I headed back to the room to get Frankie. I wanted us to get to the conference room early enough to get seats in the front.

"Oh," Frankie said slowly as she came out of the bathroom, carefully closing the door behind her. "I decided not to go." *That was a quick change of mind. Was she seasick and didn't want to tell me?*

"But we'll see him for sure," I said. She didn't look sick, but she definitely looked nervous about something. Her book was still laying in the exact same spot on the table it had been when I left, so she clearly hadn't been reading either.

"No, you go ahead," she said. "I think I'll just stay here and read."

"But you can read anytime," I said as I watched the way she sat down stiffly on the sofa. "Don't you want to at least see him in person? Don't be worried about looking like an idiot about keto. You've already read way more of his book than I have, so you know more than I do, and *I'm* still going."

"No, I'm kind of tired, too," she said.

"Okay, you may be tired," I said, "but I know when you're not telling me the whole truth. What's going on? Really?"

"Do I have to go *everywhere* with you?" she asked.

"No, you don't," I said. "But you don't have to be rude about it!" She was clearly hiding something, but I didn't have time to try to weasel the information out of her now.

I turned and stormed out of the room and headed to the conference room.

I got there while people were still filling seats, so I got as close to the front as I could. The front row seats were already taken, but I managed to get in the second row. Brake busied himself talking with a sound guy, some guy that looked like the doctor they'd touted in the newsletter. Brake's friend, the skinny guy with tiny round glasses seemed almost surgically attached to Brake's side.

I barely paid attention to the lecture. My mind kept drifting back to Frankie and why she was acting so irritable lately. It seemed like one minute she was happy and full of life—ready to take on the world—and the next she wanted to be a recluse and have nothing to do with me. I wondered if it was a mistake to have her move in with me. Of course, it was better than where she was, but what if my constant presence was getting on her nerves after living so long alone? I wasn't a psychologist, so I didn't know what the right thing would be to do. I guessed I would just have to go by her moods and give her some alone time when she wanted it.

My problem-solving thoughts got me through the long boring medical lecture and when it was finally over, people got up to mingle. I headed straight for the stage to talk to Brake at last!

But as luck would have it, his bespectacled friend stopped me before I even set foot on the first step to the stage. "No," he said flatly. "You cannot have his autograph right now."

"I don't want his autograph," I said. "I just want to talk to him." Although, as I said it, I realized that I had no idea what I would even say!

"No, he doesn't have time to answer questions right now," he said. "He's busy."

"Fine!" I said. *I'm getting my money back!* This cruise was *not* delivering what I'd paid for. I turned and stomped away. *Who knew Brake Caldwell was such a snob?*

I didn't want to go back to the room and be around Frankie, and the thought of wandering the ship by myself didn't appeal to me, but there wasn't much choice. My dinner reservations weren't until six, so I went to one of the

VIP decks and parked my sorry self in a lounger and stared at all the rich couples who seemed to have their lives all figured out. My dire retirement was stark by comparison, and I figured I'd be better off on the Lido deck with people that didn't at least make me feel guilty about my body or my wallet.

I was hurrying to the elevator when I literally bumped into Brake Caldwell. "Oh, I'm so sorry," he said, reaching out to steady me. "I know better than to run around corners! Are you okay?"

"Yes, I'm fine," I said.

"Do I *know* you?" he asked. "You look familiar."

"We met at the hotel the night before the cruise," I said.

"Oh, that's right!" he said, and his worried look almost morphed into a smile. "Philadelphia Powers."

"That's right!" *He remembered my name! He knows my name!* I wished there had been any kind of a witness around for this moment, but it was just the two of us at a corner of an empty corridor. "And you are . . . hold on, I'll think of it. Brake something or other."

He smiled and shook his head. "Don't rub it in," he said. "I know I'm not famous anymore."

"Are you kidding? Of course you are!" I said. "You're the whole reason I booked this cruise!"

"Really?" he asked. "That's sweet of you to say."

"It's true," I said. "My friend is gonna be so upset when she hears I ran into you, and she missed it again!"

"This friend," he said slowly, narrowing his eyes. "Can *other* people *see* her?"

"Yes," I said with a laugh, surprised that a celebrity could have a sense of humor. "She's not imaginary."

"She'll just have to start hanging out with you more," he said.

"That's what she promised," I said. "But as you can see, I'm on my own again."

For a second we'd run out of words. I racked my brain for anything to say to keep him here talking to me like he knew me. "Oh, I love your book, by the way!"

"Oh, you've had a chance to read it?" he asked. "Already?"

"Yes," I lied. *Why do I always lie to impress people?* "I hope you have a sequel!"

"I'm working on it," he said. "By the way, have you seen Uncle Oscar?"

"No," I said, deciding to be completely honest from now on. Not honest enough to express my glee that he'd managed to lose a guy who seemed glued to his hip, though. I remembered how back at the hotel, Brake had said he didn't dare to leave him alone too long, and I wondered if it was because of his uncle's insecurity or his own. "You lost him?"

"Yeah, I can't imagine where he's gotten to," Brake said looking totally baffled. "I've been looking everywhere."

"Well, he couldn't have gone too far," I said. "Maybe he just wants a little space, like *my* roommate."

"Maybe," he said with a half-grin. "But I don't think I'm *that* hard to live with. I think he's probably looking for me while I'm looking for him."

"That could be," I said. "Maybe we should just sit and wait for him here by the pool."

To my surprise, Brake took me up on my suggestion.

"He's just never gone off on his own like this," he said as we walked over to some loungers and sat down. "I'm getting worried."

"Oh, don't worry," I said. "Like I said, he probably just needs some space, and he'll come find you when he's ready."

"You think?" he asked.

"Yes, my friend, Frankie, is the same way," I said. "I think we just need a little time apart. Sometimes she acts like she doesn't want to be around me."

"I hope I'm not *that* bad," he said with a laugh.

"You mean *I am?*" I asked.

"No, Philadelphia," he said smiling at me. "I don't think you're bad at all."

He looked at his watch. "I've already missed my dinner reservations. Uncle Oscar is gonna get a load of my mind when he decides to come back!"

"Well, my reservation is at six," I said. "You can join me and Frankie if you want."

"Okay," he said. "Well, I'll go look in my cabin one more time to see if he came back yet and see if the butler's seen him."

"Okay, and I'll go get Frankie and meet you in the VIP restaurant," I said. "If you get there first, just ask for my table. Philadelphia Powers."

"Will do," he said.

We walked together to the elevator, and he kept heading down the corridor, so I knew he was on this floor! I hurried down to our room to get Frankie.

"Frankie!" I called as soon as I unlocked the door. The bathroom door slammed shut as soon as I opened the cabin door. *Seriously? She was that mad at me? For what?*

"Frankie! What is going on?" I demanded and knocked on the bathroom door. "Whatever it is, you need to tell me so we can fix it." Whatever it was that was causing this behavior had to be addressed *right now!* Even if it meant Brake had to wait for me.

"Just a minute," she said, not sounding mad at all,

much to my surprise.

I waited and then decided to go over and close the deck door. As soon as I closed that door the air conditioning kicked on. "Why was the door open?" I asked. "You know that when that door is open, it turns the air conditioning off. It is hot in here!"

She came out of the bathroom, carefully closing the door behind her.

"What's going on?" I asked suspiciously. "Why are you acting so weird?"

"I'm not acting weird," she said. "What's going on with you? How was the conference?"

"Oh, it was good," I said, staring at her for some kind of clue as to her odd behavior.

"Have a seat, sit down," she said, sitting on the sofa and patting the cushion beside her.

"No, we have to go to dinner," I said. "I have a surprise for you! Hurry up and get ready while I freshen up."

"No!" she shrieked as soon as my hand touched the doorknob. "Don't go in there!"

In a second, she was up and across the room, pushing me away from the door.

"Frankie, what *on earth* is going on with you?" I asked. "What's going on?"

"Nothing," she said. "You can use the bathrooms down by the restaurant."

"Seriously?" I asked. "This is my own cabin. I'm going to use the bathroom here."

"No, you can't," she said, desperately standing in front of the door with her arms stretched wide, blocking my path. "You can't go in there. Please, just don't do it." Her terrified face scared me.

"Frankie, what have you done?" I asked, trying to push her aside. "What are you hiding?"

And then it hit me. She has a *boyfriend?*

"Frankie, do you have a *man* in there?" I asked in shock. *Maybe she was more over Edgar than I'd thought!* "Is that why you won't go anywhere with me? You're seeing someone?"

"No," she said slowly and looked away, making me believe she was lying. "Not exactly."

"What do you mean not exactly?" I said. "If you've got a man in there, it's okay! If you're seeing someone, that's fine! I'm happy for you, honestly! You don't need to hide him!"

I tapped on the door. "It's okay to come out," I said.

"You wouldn't understand," she said.

"Try me," I said. "Listen, *honestly,* Frankie, it's okay. Edgar's been gone for over two years now. It's okay if you have feelings for someone else."

"Well, that's not exactly right" she said slowly with clenched teeth. "Del, I can't explain it, and I don't want you to make fun of me."

"When have I ever made fun of you?" I asked her in shock. "I said it is perfectly natural for you to have feelings for another man. You don't have to hide him."

"Well, okay, but I at least have to explain him first before you see him," she said.

My mind raced to the millions of reasons she was acting this way. "Is it a *younger* man?" I asked. "No need to be ashamed." And then it hit me. "Is it *Jeffrey?*"

"*What? No!*" she said, looking at me like I'd lost my mind. "Okay, I don't know how to say this. Don't freak out. Promise me you won't freak out."

"Frankie," I said, getting annoyed by this point. "You have three seconds to tell me or I'm gonna barge my way in there, and I don't even care if he's naked!"

"Okay, wait," she said, holding up her hands and

pushing my shoulders back. "Brace yourself."

"I'm braced," I said. "Tell me or I'm going in there."

"Okay, well, I don't know how to explain it," she hedged.

"Is it a man or not?" I asked. "Just tell me that much."

"Well, yes," she said. "And no."

"What? What do you mean by that?" I asked.

"It's kind of a man," she said. As I was about to push her aside, she blurted out. "It's Edgar!"

"What?" I shrieked. My mind raced. Edgar's dead! But is he really? She has been saying he moved! Did he leave her, and she was just too ashamed to tell me? But how did he get on this cruise? "You said he . . . he was dead."

"Well, he's back," she said. "So, just be prepared. He's . . . he's not . . . exactly the same."

Now I backed off. I had no idea what she was talking about. Was he a ghost? Had he faked his own death and now returned looking different?

"How . . . *is* he?" I asked carefully.

"Well, do you believe in an afterlife?" she asked. "Like reincarnation?"

"I don't know," I said carefully. "Are you telling me you've trapped some man in the bathroom and won't let him out because you think it's Edgar?" I was seriously worried about her mental health.

"Not exactly," she said. "He came here on his own. I was talking to Edgar, telling him how much I missed him and wishing he could send me a sign . . . and then, he just showed up at my door. See for yourself."

Now I didn't dare open the bathroom door. I was terrified of what I would find. Some strange man who had been pulled in and locked in the bathroom? A ghost?

Whatever it was, I had to know. I reached out with trepidation and turned the door handle, slowly opening it in case whoever was in there was going to try to get revenge and grab me.

I didn't see anything, so I pushed it open further, and there, sitting in the middle of our VIP bathroom, was a *dog!* I let out an involuntary breath I hadn't realized I'd been holding. "Oh, for Pete's sake!" I said in exasperation. "It's a dog!"

"Yes, it's *Edgar,*" she said. "Come on, Edgar." The dog obediently walked straight to her and then after a quick pat went directly to Frankie's bed and jumped up on it and laid down on her—or *his*—pajamas!

"It's *not* Edgar," I told her, still shaking from the suspense of thinking a strange man or ghost could be in the bathroom. "It's just a dog."

"But I was talking to Edgar," she said. "I asked him for a sign, and then I heard a noise outside my door. I opened it, thinking you forgot your key or something. When I opened it, there he was. He walked right in and jumped right up on my bed. *Right on his pajamas!* It's *him*, Del! I know it's him!"

I was speechless, both at her desperate delusion and the fact that there was a fricken *dog sitting in the middle of a bed in a cabin—in the middle of the ocean!*

"You can't breathe a word of it to anyone," she said, sitting down and hugging the dog. "They'll take him away."

"Frankie, he has to belong to *someone,*" I said.

"On a cruise?" she asked. "I don't think dogs are allowed on a cruise."

I didn't know about that, seeing a how there *was* one—and he had to come from *somewhere!* "We have to report that you found him," I said. "Someone might be missing him."

"If so, there would be an announcement or something," she said. "If it's in the daily newsletter or something, then I'll report it, but he could've just gotten on by accident when everyone boarded. He might've snuck in with the luggage somehow."

She wrapped her arms around the dog and the dog snuggled up to her.

"Okay, so let me get this straight," I said. "You're going to stay *here* with a dog that doesn't belong to you while I go have dinner with *Brake Caldwell?*"

She looked shocked at that news. After a brief hesitation she nodded. "Yes," she said. "I'll be ordering in for me and Edgar. You have your date, and I'll have mine."

Chapter 18: Dinner and a Dog

My flabbergastedness was still evident on my face when I reached the restaurant and made my way to the table. Brake was already there.

"Is something wrong?" he asked.

"My friend, Frankie, is . . . something else," I said. I remembered her desperate plea to keep her secret, and I couldn't betray that, but she was beginning to drive me around the bend. "She's grieving over her late husband, and I guess you could say she has ups and downs."

"I see," he said. "And this is obviously a down."

"More like a sideways," I said. "So, I guess it's just you and me. Any luck with your Uncle Oscar?"

"No, no one's seen him," he said. "I hope he didn't fall overboard."

"I think there's security or something that prevents that," I said. "And if anyone fell overboard, I'm sure someone would announce 'man overboard' or something, right?"

"I would hope so," he said but still looked worried.

"Well, try not to worry," I said. "It will probably do you some good to have a break from him. I'm sure he can take care of himself."

"Yeah," Brake finally said with a lopsided grin, making him look familiar again. It was the old him when he smiled. The one I'd had plastered all over my bedroom walls and kissed every night before going to sleep. *Now here I was—having dinner with him!* "I mean, how far could he go, right? He's probably just out exploring the ship and having a blast."

"That's what I think," I said. "Just enjoy your free evening."

"So, Philadelphia Powers," he said, after the waiter took our orders. "Tell me about *you.*"

I told him about my meagre social security check and my Never-Got-To-Do list. I even shared the embarrassing story about my stint as a background actor.

He laughed. "It's true what they said," he said. "I fainted my first time on set. Those lights are hot!"

I liked it that we had something in common. And then—there he was. *Uncle Oscar—the bespectacled beanpole that didn't want me anywhere near Brake.* I saw him come in and crane his neck, obviously looking for Brake. I knew our date was over now.

"Well, there he is," I said with a tone of resignation.

"Who?" Brake asked and looked behind him.

"Your Uncle Oscar," I said.

"Where!" he said and stood up so he could see better. Apparently, he was blind because the man was walking right towards us.

"Right there!" I said as the guy approached.

"Paul! Where's Uncle Oscar?" he asked him. Clearly this bespectacled sidekick was *Paul.*

"We can't find him," Paul said. "I've got all the butlers and ship's security now looking for him."

"Oh my heavens!" I said, shocked that I'd thought Brake's uncle was *this guy* when he was probably some little old man that was lost somewhere. "Maybe we *should* go look for him."

"Security and all the ship's crew are looking for him

now," Paul said. "There isn't really anything else we can do."

Brake looked at me. "I thought you said you saw him."

"I was mistaken," I said sheepishly.

"Okay, I just wanted to let you know," Paul said. "I'll let you get back to your date."

I waited for Brake to clarify that it *wasn't* a date—*but he didn't!* My heart soared. If he didn't deny it, then it *was* a date! *I was officially on a date with Brake Caldwell!* My lifelong dream had come true! I could definitely check this one off the Never-Got-To-Do list!

"So, Philadelphia Powers," he said with a grin after our meal was served. "What's next on your Never-Got-To-Do list?"

"Okay, please just stop using my full name," I said. "Just call me Del."

He chuckled. "I get that all the time," he said. "People come up to me and address me by my full name all the time. It sounds weird to me."

I wondered if I'd done that when I'd met him at the hotel. I couldn't remember if I had or not. I probably had. That was me.

"So? What else do you have to check off?" he asked.

"I have yet to ride in a limo, walk the red carpet, sign autographs, and publish a book," I said.

"Well, I can help with at least one of those," he said.

"Yeah?"

"Yeah, they'll be sending a limo for me tomorrow when we dock in Hawaii," he said. "You're welcome to join me. We're probably all booked at the same hotel anyway."

"Okay!" I readily agreed.

"And your friend too," he said. "If she'll agree to leave the room—if she really exists, that is!"

"Of course she's real," I said with a laugh, glad that Brake was comfortable enough to joke around with me.

"Okay, just asking," he said. "I'm still not convinced she's not just your imaginary friend."

"Well, there's a reason," I said. For some reason, I felt like I could trust him. Probably because I felt like I'd known him all my life. "I will tell you, if you promise never to tell anyone at all."

"Cross my heart," he said, swiping his index finger across his chest in a big x. "Tell me, tell me." His grin was contagious.

"Okay, well, she thinks her dead husband has reincarnated into a dog," I explained, realizing how absurd it sounded even as the words came out of my mouth.

"What? That's . . .different," he said. I could see his face change as his mind obviously rolled through a string of words to find the least offensive version of what he was thinking. "Why would she think that?"

"When I was out today, she was apparently talking to her dead husband and heard a noise at the cabin door. When she opened it, there was a dog. She'd been asking her dead husband for a sign, so she not only took that as a sign *from* him—but now thinks he's been reincarnated into this dog. He walked right in, jumped up on her bed, and lied down on her husband's pajamas. She really, honestly believes it's him. She doesn't want anyone to know because she doesn't know what they'll do to the dog. He probably just got on somehow by accident in Los Angeles."

He let out a long breath. "You're kidding!"

"No," I said. "I swear! It's true! A real live dog."

"Describe it," he said in an even tone with his eyes closed, so I did. He opened his eyes and stared at me. *"That is Uncle Oscar!"*

"What?" I was shocked.

"I've been talking for *hours* about how my dog is missing, and you didn't think to tell me that your friend found a random lost dog?" he asked, staring at me like I was denser than the table.

"How was *I* to know that your Uncle Oscar was a *dog?*" I asked.

"You *said* you read my book!" he exclaimed. "I believed you! There are two entire chapters in there all about Uncle Oscar and how much he'd helped me when I was grieving my dad!"

I was mortified. "I'm *so* sorry!" I said. "I didn't actually *get to that part* yet!"

"It was the *second and third* chapters!" Brake stared at me like I was an imbecile—which, to be honest, I felt like in that moment.

"Okay, look, I didn't *actually* get a chance to read your book yet," I said, watching him as he put his napkin beside his dinner and stood up.

"I need to get my dog back," he said. "I was worried sick."

I could tell he was upset with me for not being honest about reading his book. Or perhaps it was because he thought I'd been hiding his dog.

"Well, he's in a safe place with my friend," I said. "We could finish dinner and go get him afterwards."

"No, I want to go *now,*" he said firmly. "I can't be sure your friend even really exists!" This time it wasn't a playful joke. This time there was no smile.

"What, you think I just decided to kidnap your dog and lock him up in my cabin?" I had no choice but to go with him. "Look, I'm sorry I lied about reading your book," I said as we walked to the elevator.

"Everybody lies," he said flatly.

"Not *everybody,*" I said. "*I* normally don't! Well,

I might embellish from time to time, but I don't try to lie. I honestly didn't know he was your dog. I would've never just stolen a celebrity's dog."

"Look, stans do all kinds of weird things, including stealing celebrities' dogs," he said. "But you, with your quirky name and your Never-Got-To-Do list—I thought you just might be the *first* authentic person I'd met in a long time. Silly me. Let's go get my dog."

"Okay, look," I said while I had him as a captive listener. "I don't know what a stan is but—"

"It's a stalker fan," he said flatly, not even looking at me. "Give me my dog and stay away from me."

We stepped into the elevator in silence and rode it up to my floor. When I opened the door, Frankie was lying on her bed with Uncle Oscar, reading Brake's book.

"Frankie, I have some bad news," I said as Brake followed me into the room.

She sat up and her eyes widened at the sight of Brake. *"Brake Caldwell!"* she said.

"Um, Frankie," I said. "I don't know how to tell you this, but *that* isn't Edgar."

"I know, Del," she said, holding up Brake's book. "I just got to that chapter. I'm so sorry, Brake. I just got to the part where Uncle Oscar came into your life after your father died."

Brake seemed to soften when he saw Frankie's sad face, and I could tell he knew exactly what it felt like to grieve so deeply.

"Uncle Oscar," he said. "Come here, boy!"

The dog obediently leapt from the bed and rushed to Brake's arms.

"I'm sorry," I said. "We honestly didn't know it was your dog."

He hesitated for a moment and shrugged.

"Of course it was silly of me to think it was Edgar," Frankie said, rubbing her husband's pajamas, probably still warm from where the dog had just been lying on them.

"I understand you're grieving too," he said to her. I wasn't sure if he was being kind or just checking to see if I'd lied about Frankie too.

She nodded silently. Surprisingly, Uncle Oscar leaped from Brake's arms and dashed back to Frankie, jumping up beside her and licking her cheek.

"Oh, no, Uncle Oscar," Frankie said. "You have to go home with your daddy now! Yes, you do! Oh yes you do! I know I said that you are my husband, but we just had a little misunderstanding, didn't we?"

Brake watched in amusement as she spoke in babytalk to Uncle Oscar. At least he could obviously see that I hadn't made up the part about Frankie thinking Uncle Oscar was Edgar reincarnated!

"Well, I suppose it wouldn't hurt if Uncle Oscar sleeps here for one night," Brake said. "He's a good therapist."

"Really?" Frankie looked at Brake in surprise, and I could tell she was trying not to cry. So was I.

"I'll pick him up in the morning." Brake nodded and left the room.

"So, I had a date with a celebrity," I said to her, trying to lighten the mood for both of us. "And you had a date with his dog."

She laughed. "Old Uncle Oscar and I are becoming fast friends," she said.

"Well, I'm going to go for a walk, I think," I said. "I need to just get out and get some fresh air." I left Frankie reading with Uncle Oscar, and I went back up to the pool. I needed time to myself for once to sort out my feelings.

I was too afraid of heights to actually look over the

rail at the water, but I did discover I was able to stand at the rail and survey the Lido deck several stories below me. For some reason I felt too sad to be afraid of heights completely at the moment.

What was wrong with me? I searched my soul for answers as to why I always seemed to exaggerate things. Why do I have such a hard time just simply stating what is? What is it I'm afraid of?

My heart answered. I'm afraid I'm not enough as I am. If I show there's something I don't know, I'll appear weak. I had to be the problem solver. I couldn't afford to not know something. I couldn't afford not to have a solution. I'd become so accustomed to thinking outside the box, the box didn't even exist anymore.

I wanted to change but I didn't know how. I couldn't *stop* being a problem solver when I had so many problems that needed solving. The most nagging one being that I'd spent way more money than I could afford on this cruise. I needed to figure a way to solve that.

I was also annoyed with myself for lying about reading Brake's book. And then it hit me. If *he* was making a fortune from *his* book, maybe *I* could write my own book about my adventures and make money from that! I did have "*publish a book*" on my Never-Got-To-Do list!

I pulled out my phone and did some calculations. If I did background acting a few times a week, I'd earn enough for the minimum credit card payments each month, and in the meantime, I'd write a book. And I *needed* it to be a bestseller!

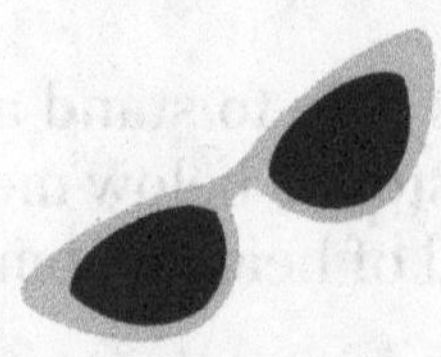

Chapter 19: A Free Drink

I had one more day to make things right with Brake. In the morning, we would be disembarking in Hawaii for three days. Hawaii was big, and I knew I'd be unlikely to see him there.

I went up to the pool and looked around. My heart raced as soon as I saw Uncle Oscar sitting loyally beside his chair. The chairs were facing away from me so all I could see of Brake were his tanned elbows resting on the armrests.

"Brake!" I called. I couldn't keep the words from spilling out as I marched full speed towards the back of his chair. I had a word or two to get off my chest before I was going to let some washed-up has-been call *me* a liar and just walk away! "Listen, here, mister! You have no right to accuse me of stealing your dog and just walking away without giving me a chance to explain!"

I came around his chair to face him now, everything pouring out a mile a minute. "I was willing to give you the benefit of the doubt because I thought you were a pretty decent guy! But seriously, you knew I'd *just* bought the book, and if you thought I was going to stay up all night the night before a cruise, reading a three-inch-thick book, then you're more delusional about our relationship than I am! And it should be easy for you to see how I could get confused between a dog and your psycho-control-freak handler!"

I watched his jaw drop. Then I noticed that it wasn't Brake's jaw. In fact, it wasn't Brake's *face!* It was the other half of that beautiful couple from the port terminal. And then I felt the sting of the cold smell of alcohol as it slapped me in the face.

"Get away from my husband, you hussy!" It was his beautiful wife who looked like she actually thought she could throw physical daggers from her eyes.

I stood there with my mouth open and my face wet, blinking back the shock from my mistake and the cold drink. "I, I'm sorry," I managed to somehow cough out. "I didn't know—"

"Well, you know *now!*" she shouted. "You stay away from my husband unless you want me to throw you overboard!"

"Wow, that's an extreme reaction," I said. "It was a mistake. I didn't mean—"

"You're *right* it was a mistake, you old bag!" she said. "Go find your own man and leave mine alone!"

I was unable to lower my eyebrows as I stiffly walked away in shock and embarrassment. I wanted to apologize to the man again, but I didn't dare say another word to him because I didn't doubt his crazed wife would actually try to throw me overboard. Although she had no idea what *I'd* be doing while she was trying to do that! But to be honest, I didn't either.

In shame I headed toward the exit, anxious to go hide in my room after making such a humiliating public display.

"I take it that was meant for me," a familiar voice said behind me.

I didn't answer. I was humiliated.

"Look," Brake said calmly as I reached the elevator and tapped my card. He followed me in. "I heard what you said. I get it. But to be fair, Paul was helping me try to find Uncle Oscar who'd gone missing since I boarded the ship. I was in a panic thinking he somehow got off the ship before we left port."

I couldn't speak. I got off the elevator and headed straight for my room.

"As you can see, Uncle Oscar goes wherever he wants," he said, following me. "Today he just happened to attach himself to the poor victim of your tirade."

"Look," I said as I reached my door. "I'm sorry for mistaking your dog for your—Paul! It's none of my business. I shouldn't have been stalking you. I will stay away from you."

I tapped my card on the lock.

"Now, let's don't get hasty!" he said calmly. "It's been years since I've had a genuine stalker. And for the record, I wouldn't expect *anyone* to pull an all-nighter reading *my* book. And as stalkers go, I do admire your dedication."

I opened the door and walked in, allowing the door to close in his grinning face. I was through with celebrities! I didn't care if I ever saw one again.

"Where have *you* been?" Frankie asked, coming in from the deck, her book in hand.

"Giving a complete stranger a piece of my mind that I couldn't afford to lose," I said.

"Oh, so a regular Friday then, right?" she asked and laughed.

I couldn't help smiling a little. She was right, I guessed. "Well, it wasn't fair for Brake to just accuse me of trying to manipulate him into liking me."

"But, Del," she said with one raised eyebrow. "That's exactly what you *did*."

"Oh, shut up," I said in a playful-but-really-annoyed

way. "You were, too. And when he was going on about losing his uncle, how was *I* to know he meant his *dog?*"

"Yeah, but look," she held up the book and pointed to Brake's picture on the back cover. "If you'd paid attention to even the cover of the book, you'd have seen the dog with him in his author photo. And if you read the author bio, you'd have read that his trusted companion is his dog, affectionately named Uncle Oscar."

I hated that she was right and proud of it—especially since it all started with *her* taking the dog! I wanted to say, *yeah, well at least I didn't think it was my dead husband!* But I didn't. Even in my state of shame and frustration, I wasn't about to be cruel to my best friend.

"Well, live and learn," I said. "I need a shower." Not just to wash that crazy woman's drink off me, but to wash away my humiliation. To clean off the insanity of stalking a washed-up movie star. I clearly would never travel in his circles. Just being able to live a floor below him for eight days had cost me more than several months' rent, and I was growing increasingly worried about my credit card being declined at the end of the trip from racking up so many extra expenses.

As the water washed away the grime of my delusion, I vowed that from this point out, this cruise would be what it was supposed to be. Frankie and me living our dreams and enjoying life to the fullest. I promised myself that Hawaii would be the dream luxury resort experience that Frankie and I had fantasized about for years. I owed it to her. I also owed it to myself.

Chapter 20: Peace and Friendship

Hawaii turned out to be the old times we'd been trying to recapture. Frankie and I reveled in our spacious luxury hotel room overlooking the Pacific Ocean and miles of long white sandy beaches, filled with tiny colorful dots of people.

"To the beach!" Frankie declared as she came out of the bathroom in her bathing suit with a sheer peach cotton cover-up. Her oversized pink sunglasses and straw sunhat told me she was embracing the joy.

"Oh, I didn't bring a sunhat," I thought, wondering how she'd managed to fit that into her suitcase without it getting crumpled.

"Oh, I bought this in the gift shop on the ship," she said. "Try saying *that* fast five times! But you can probably buy one here in the hotel gift shop."

I hated the niggling feeling that she was wasting my money. I tried to push it down. "Are the sunglasses new?"

"Yes, do you like them?" she asked.

"Yes," I said, trying to sound enthusiastic and not think about the money. *We're here to have fun!* I kept telling myself that. "I'll have to get some."

So, I fought off the financial demon on my shoulder and we stopped at the gift shop on our way down to the beach. I kept focusing on my promise to myself. *I'm not going to waste this luxurious experience worrying about the future! I'm going to live in the moment!* If Frankie could manage to do it, then I could do it too! I'd sort out the money later!

So, with matching gigantic sunhats, we settled into two beach loungers under huge umbrellas with cool drinks and happy hearts. The sun warmed me inside and out, and the sound of the crashing waves and happy beachgoers relaxed me.

"This is the life," Frankie said beside me and took a sip of her drink. "I never thought I'd ever get to do this."

"Me neither," I said. "But I'm glad we did." And I was. Maybe when we got home, I'd have money problems, but right here—*right now*—I had sun, sand, and surf.

"I can't believe you actually went on a date with a celebrity," she said, taking another drink. "I've never seen anyone more determined to cross anything off a list before." It was good to hear her laugh.

"Let's just not mention his name ever again," I said. "I'm *done* with celebrities. I guess sitting down with the *intention* to have dinner can count as a date, so I will cross it off, because let's just say I'm done with pursuing *that* goal."

"I'm just going to relax and enjoy this peace," Frankie said, settling back and pulling her sunhat lower over her eyes.

"Frankie," I tapped her arm and whispered. "Look, that's them."

The beautiful couple from the terminal—and my disastrous tirade—were trudging through the sand in our direction. The man was waving his hands around, which was the most movement I'd ever seen from him, while the woman was ineffectively stomping through the sand. I could hear her grating voice before they got close enough for me to hear his.

"I don't know what you're talking about!" she yelled, spraying sand in all directions as she stomped furiously ahead of her husband.

"Oh, you know perfectly well what I'm saying!" he said as they got even closer to us. "You're a control freak. Everyone else can see it! Even little old ladies! You never even let me have my own opinion about anything!"

"Well, you're having an opinion now!" she yelled as they stomped past our loungers—oblivious to us *little old ladies*—and carried on in the direction of the hotel.

"I'm just tired of it!" he shouted. "You tell me what to do all the time, and I don't have any say at all in *any* part of my own life!"

After they were out of earshot, I explained to Frankie in full detail what had happened by the pool. "So," I said in conclusion. "I think it's my fault they're fighting. Maybe I should go and try to apologize and explain what was *really* going on and how I mistook that guy for Brake."

"Let it go," Frankie advised. "It's clear they were already having problems. Otherwise, they would've just laughed it off and been done with it. Maybe you gave him the courage to stand up for himself."

"Maybe," I said thoughtfully.

"I guess it goes to show that money doesn't solve everything," Frankie said.

"Maybe not *everything*," I agreed. "But it would definitely help pay off my credit card!"

"We'll probably have to do some background acting when we get home," she said calmly. "I'll help you pay on it since it was for me too."

I felt a little better knowing that she was being conscientious about the money too, and I could finally relax a little more.

At the end of three days, we made our way back to

the ship, tanned, tired, yet rejuvenated. This trip had been good for the both of us.

We were settled in and just about ready to get into our pajamas when a frantic knock came to the door.

"It must be the butler," I said. "Who else could it be?" I hoped it wasn't that guy I'd yelled at by the pool! Or his wife!

But it wasn't any of those people. I opened the door to see Brake standing there with an odd expression. "Yes?" I said flatly, not inviting him in.

"I thought Frankie might want to say goodbye to Uncle Oscar," he said, and I watched as tears welled up in his eyes.

"Oh my gosh, what happened?" Frankie hurried across the room to the door.

"Well, Uncle Oscar was old," he said with a quivering lip. "*Is* old. He's 23 years old, and I guess that's pretty old for a dog. He's been slowing down and acting a lot quieter lately. Anyway, he's with the ship's vet right now, and we don't expect him to make it through the night. So, if you want to come say goodbye, where he was attached to you, it might be good for him."

"Sure, of course!" Frankie said. "Come on, Del!"

"If it's okay with you?" I asked Brake. I didn't know if he was only extending an invitation to Frankie or not, but I didn't want her to have to deal with another death all by herself.

"Of course," he said. "Come on."

The three of us hurried down the corridor and into the elevator. I wanted to reach out and hug Brake because he suddenly looked so lost and helpless. He was no longer the larger-than-life star that had lived on my bedroom wall as a teenager. Now here he was, a heartbroken man made of flesh and blood.

The vet left us alone with Uncle Oscar, who lay there, his breathing slow and faint.

"I'm so sorry," Frankie said as she made her way around to the opposite side of the table, looking as though she were about to cry as she stroked Oscar's head. "Hey, Uncle Oscar, it's me. Frankie." She held her face down close to his.

I stood behind Brake on the opposite side while he draped his arm across Uncle Oscar's middle. I felt like I didn't belong there. I wasn't grieving for the dog I didn't even know, but my heart was breaking for the two people who were crying for Uncle Oscar. I reached out and rested my hand on Brake's shoulder. It was the only kind of support I was able to give. It was then that I realized that Brake's decision to come and get us probably had more to do with his need not to go through this alone. I firmly stood behind him, so he knew he didn't have to.

In the early hours of the morning, Uncle Oscar moved to heaven with one final breath that seemed like a sigh of peace, as if he knew he was loved right up until the very end. Frankie and I waited while Brake hugged his faithful companion and sobbed into his fur. We waited silently, giving him the space he needed until finally, Frankie bent over his shoulder and whispered, "Let us walk you back." She was the only one who could know what he needed at that moment.

As we slowly walked the hall to Brake's door, I reached out and slipped my hand into his. Not so I could say I'd held the hand of a celebrity, but because it was all I had to offer solace.

"We can stay if you need us to," I offered when we reached his place.

"I would appreciate that," he said. So, he invited us into his lavish penthouse that was the size of an apartment. I tried not to detract from his moment by gushing over his accommodations.

His butler made coffee for us and then left us alone. None of us could drink anything. Frankie and I sat on either side of Brake with our arms draped across his back, as he leaned forward with his head in his hands.

"He's been with me since my father died twelve years ago," he said.

"I know," Frankie said. "But like you said in your book, animals come to us when we need them and leave us only when they feel we are strong enough to handle life without them."

"But I'm not!" he said. "I can't *imagine* life without him!"

"Well, you have *us* now," I said. I didn't have all the backstory that Frankie had, and I felt a little jealous about that, but my heart went out to Brake. Even without knowing anything at all about the real him. And not just because he was a celebrity, but because he was a hurting human being who had just lost a friend he loved. I realized how one-dimensional I'd held him in my mind all these years. It was clear I'd been in love with a fictional human being, and I was just beginning to meet the real person.

The three of us wept together with intermittent words from Brake and murmurs of consolation from Frankie and me. Seeing Frankie able to console someone else while she was still coping with her own grief gave me hope that she was getting stronger and moving forward.

"I've been living on this ship for three years," he said. "My parents are gone. I have no family left. I never married or had kids. I literally have no place to go and no place to bury Uncle Oscar."

I was shocked by this admission. For all his fame and wealth, Brake Caldwell was as lost and alone as the rest of us. I hated myself for having called him a washed-up has-been, and I couldn't remember if I'd been cruel enough to say that to his face, or to that beautiful woman's husband, or if it had been something I'd kept inside my head. With me it was hard to tell, so I just hoped I'd had some measure of control previously.

"We're here for you," was all I could say. I wondered what the vet had done with Uncle Oscar's body.

By the time Brake was exhausted enough to sleep, Frankie and I went back to our room. Ironically, we now knew where Brake lived—and it didn't matter the way it had mattered when we didn't know. And I could legitimately say I was his friend now. I understood now that *being* a friend was more than just *having* a friend.

Chapter 21: Plans and a Plot

In the morning, we went to see if Brake wanted to join us for breakfast, but his butler said he was sleeping and didn't want to be disturbed, so Frankie and I went to the dining room without him.

"It's a shame for him," Frankie said. "I wish we could help him feel better."

"I know," I said. "Me too." Frankie was going through the same thing I'd been going through with her. Painfully watching her grieve and being helpless to fix it.

After breakfast I asked Jeffrey, "What happens if there's a death on the ship?" I was thinking maybe special arrangements had to be made to airlift the body somewhere, and with Brake not having anywhere to send Uncle Oscar, I didn't know what would happen.

"We have a morgue on the ship for when people die during the cruise," he said.

"People *die* on *cruises?*" I shrieked. "Like, normally? Is it common?"

"People die *everywhere*," he admitted. "A lot of guests are older or unwell. For some it's their last hoorah when they know they're dying."

"Ew!" I said without thinking. "I mean, how awful. So, you mean, there are *dead bodies* somewhere on this ship *right now?*"

"I don't have *that* information," he said. Something told me that even if he *had* had that information, he was not about to share it with guests. "But there is nothing to worry about. The morgue is way below deck. No one has access to it but the medical staff."

"What about dogs?" I asked.

"Yes," he said with a nod. "Dog's too."

"Okay, we have to do something to help Brake," I said to Frankie as we went back up to our room.

"Like what?" she asked. "There is nothing *we* can do."

"Maybe there is," I said. "Come on."

We went back up to Brake's room and his butler still refused to let us in. "It's important," I said, not willing to take no for an answer this time. He left us standing in the hall while he went to check with Brake and then allowed us inside. He directed us to the seating area. "Brake will be with you shortly."

"What are you going to do?" Frankie asked, eyeing me suspiciously.

"I'm not a hundred percent sure yet," I said. "First I'll find out what Brake wants."

Brake came out from his bedroom in a housecoat and pajama pants and sat across from us in a deep beige armchair. "Good morning, ladies," he said, but his face still looked sad, and it was not a good morning at all.

"I have an idea," I began immediately. "Listen, you said you had no place to bury Uncle Oscar, right?"

"That's right," he said. His face was emotionless.

"Well, what if I found a grave for him?" I asked.

"What? How will you do that?" he asked.

"Well, I know of an empty grave that my daughter bought for me, that I sold to my dead husband's mistress by accident," I said. "I can't think of a more deserving loved one than Uncle Oscar. What if I could get that back for him?"

"Okay, that would be amazing," he said. "But you said you sold it?"

"Yes, but if I'm right about this, I bet anything she would willingly donate it to Uncle Oscar," I said.

"Really?" he asked.

"Really?" Frankie repeated.

"Yes!" I insisted. "As long as we don't tell her Uncle Oscar is a dog! Look, Brake, whether you realize it or not, every woman our age once had your poster all over her bedroom walls as a teenager—even my ex-husband's mistress! I'm almost sure she was human once, so I would bet anything that she would not only sell the grave back to me, but she'd probably donate it freely, complete with the casket and headstone just have her name in the paper next to *the* Brake Caldwell! Heck, she'd probably dig the grave with her bare hands!"

"But would the cemetery *allow* a dog to be buried there?" he asked, and I could see that his stubborn common sense couldn't grasp the magic of possibilities yet.

"They don't have to *know* he's a dog," I said. "We can have the hearse deliver the casket to the ship, and we can put Uncle Oscar in it. It never has to be opened at the grave site, and no one would even know!"

"You actually think Fred's *soulmate* would let *you* have it back?" Frankie asked me.

"She doesn't have to know I have anything to do with it," I said.

"How will you manage that?" Frankie wanted to know.

"If you *can* manage that," Brake said. "I don't know how I would thank you!"

"No thanks needed," I said. "That's what friends are for! Let me work on it."

But I was *already* working on it and the plan was

nearly completely formed in my mind. "Just do me a favor and write up what you would like the headstone to say, okay?"

He shrugged and slowly shook his head. "You're fantastic, Philadelphia, you know that?"

I smiled and realized he was probably just speaking from his heartbreak over Uncle Oscar. "Do you have a computer, by any chance?"

He led us over to a little desk with a laptop on it, "be my guest."

I sat down and his butler served us coffee. "Okay," I said, opening a Word document. "Let's write a press release!" I read it aloud when I finished it.

For Immediate Release:
Famed Celebrity Brake Caldwell Seeks Burial Plot in Davenport!
Brake Caldwell, known for his many movies throughout the 80s and 90s, will be visiting Davenport for an extended stay following the death of his beloved Uncle Oscar. He is seeking to purchase a burial plot within the city, preferably overlooking the ocean, since Uncle Oscar spent his last three years at sea.

"He was my best friend, and I miss him terribly," the actor has said after the shocking news. Caldwell has been on a whirlwind book tour that he is cutting short because of the death in the family.

Should anyone have a plot they would wish to sell, Brake Caldwell has stated that price is no object.

"Well, what do you guys think?" I asked.

"You do know you're volunteering *his* money to purchase the plot, right?" Frankie asked.

"Oh, I don't mind!" Brake said quickly. "Of course,

I'll pay whatever she wants for it! Price really is no object!"

"Trust me, she isn't even going to want to charge anything for it," I said.

"But what if she doesn't even see this?" Frankie asked.

"Oh, she'll see it," I said. "Because I'll also throw in there that this celebrity also plans on visiting the Ross Museum, *owned* by Mrs. Ross while he's in the city. That way, if she doesn't see it herself, all her friends will show her!"

"How do you know she owns a museum?" Frankie asked.

"When I sold the plot to her daughter, I googled her name just to make sure I wasn't meeting up with some criminal or something, and I found out about all her family's businesses."

"This is amazing!" Brake said in awe. "Del, you're amazing!" It was the first time he'd called me Del without me having to tell him to.

"Now, if I know what Mrs. Ross is like, and I believe I do since she obviously has no boundaries—seeing as how she thought *my* husband was *her* soulmate—she will jump at this just to get her name in the paper," I said.

We had to use Frankie's email address because I didn't want her to recognize my name and certainly didn't want her to have *Brake's* personal email address—which I didn't even have!

I sent the news release off to every radio and news station in Davenport, along with both newspapers.

"By the time we dock in three days, we should have the burial plot," I said.

"If we don't," Brake said. "I can just purchase a plot in Davenport anyway. That is if you'd like to have me around for a while. I mean, the thought of getting back on this ship without Uncle Oscar is just too hard right now."

"Of course!" I said, my heart leaping at the thought of him actually wanting to hang out with us—*in public!* "We have a spare bedroom! You could stay with us!"

"And we could move all the craft stuff into the living room," Frankie said.

"And you can put all your things in storage," I suggested to Brake.

"Are you guys sure?" he said. "I mean, I *can* stay in a hotel, you know."

"But why bother?" I said, knowing that it wouldn't be good for him to be alone right now. "Right now, you need to be with friends. It's not good to be alone."

"Trust me," said Frankie. "I've been there. It's a really hard rut to dig yourself out of. Even with an amazing friend like Del."

I blushed and grabbed her hand.

"So, you'll do it?" I asked.

"I'm just living one day at a time, right now," he said. "If you want me to, I will."

"I do!" I said. And I meant it from the bottom of my heart.

Chapter 22: Brake and Del

Just in case Mrs. Ross's response didn't happen quickly enough, I sent an email from my phone to a Davenport Vet and made arrangements to have Uncle Oscar kept in their morgue until we could get him buried. I would have to talk to Brake in the morning about the costs, since it was his dog and ultimately his obligation. Especially since he had way more money than I did.

I couldn't sleep. I tried to quiet the scenarios racing through my mind as Frankie slept in the bed across from me. I noticed she wasn't snoring anymore. I stared at her for a minute to make sure she was still alive and was relieved when her silhouette slowly rose and fell in a slow but steady rhythm.

I tossed and turned as I envisioned how Uncle Oscar's burial could happen. *Could we really get away with burying a dog between Fred and the Rosses?* I figured we *had* to get away with it, because unlike Mrs. Ross, I wasn't keen on having my name in the papers, and if this didn't go according to plan, I probably would be in the news everywhere.

I tossed and turned and finally got up. I just couldn't lay there any longer and watch the various successful—and unsuccessful scenarios—play out in my head. I quietly got dressed and headed up to the pool.

The humid night felt like a hug and even with the lights from the ship, the millions of stars in the sky seemed to dance to the music from the deck below. I went to the rail to look down on the Lido Deck. At four in the morning, there were *still* people eating and dancing and swimming and laughing. And here I stood, just above them, on my dream cruise, alone and worried. I released a sigh that felt like it was taking all the problems of the world off my shoulders, only it didn't.

"That was a deep sigh," Brake's voice said gently from behind me. I whirled around.

"What are you doing here?" I asked. "It's four in the morning!"

"I know," he said. "What are *you* doing up this late?"

"I couldn't sleep," I admitted.

"Me neither," he admitted and pointed back to a lounger with a blanket on it. "I've been sleeping there. I can't bear to sleep in my bed without Uncle Oscar."

"I'm sorry," I said. I wished I had some words of wisdom to bestow, but I didn't. It wasn't like Uncle Oscar had pajamas that Brake could wear. "I don't know what to say. I've never really been attached to a pet." If truth were told, I'd never been attached to *anything* except my daughter. Not after Fred. I'd never let myself open up like that to that kind of heartbreak again. I'd been self-sufficient, and it had worked out well for me. I could take care of myself—and anyone else that needed it.

"I always said if anything happened to him, I'd never get another pet," Brake said. He leaned against the railing with me and looked down at the happy people below us. "It's amazing how people can be in the same place and going through such different emotions."

"I know," I said, watching the people below us portray the image of what a cruise is supposed to be. "It seems there's always something to celebrate, even if we aren't participating."

"Yeah, that's the way of life, isn't it?" he said thoughtfully. "It just goes on, no matter whether we can keep up or not."

I thought about Frankie and how life had gone on without her for two whole years.

We stood in silence, each in our own thoughts. Out of the blue, he placed his hand on top of mine.

"I don't know what I would do without you, Del," he said quietly. "You came into my life like the Tasmanian devil, and now it's that fiery spirit of yours that is keeping me from the brink of despair. Somehow you always make me feel like there's a solution to everything. Even death."

"Actually, if you recall, I actually came into your life by minding my own business," I pointed out. "I was just sitting there, reading a book, minding my own business, and you approached me!"

"I stand corrected," he said quietly. "However it happened, I'm thankful it did."

I didn't know what to say. It was clear that his dog had been his only friend for a while, and now it seemed like he was just transferring that need for friendship onto me. Weeks ago, I would've taken his friendship any way I could get it. But now it was different. Now I didn't see him as a famous star, but as a friend who needed me. I could be there for him in his time of need, but I was not going to allow it to go to my head or allow myself to get too attached. It was one thing when he was just a fun challenge to check off a list, but now he was *real*. A tangible human being with emotions that I couldn't allow myself to hurt— or allow to hurt me.

We stood in silence for a little while. I figured maybe he didn't really require a response from me as much as he needed me to just listen. Just to be there. I could do that. He still held my hand, and I wasn't going to push it away.

"You know," he said after some thought. "When my father passed away, I thought it was the end of my world. Then Uncle Oscar found me. I spent months talking to him about my father."

I waited, still unsure of what to say, so I just listened.

"My father was a doctor," he said with a faint smile. "His writing was so bad, like a typical doctor, that when he filled out my birth registration, it was interpreted as Brake when it was supposed to be Blake."

"Oh, that's hilarious," I said. "Sort of the same thing happened to me."

"Let me guess," he said with a half-smile, almost as if he could forget for a split second that his dog had just died. "Your father was registering his place of birth."

"No," I said with a laugh. "I was named Philadelphia on purpose because my parents were there on a business trip when I decided to be born early. They said I was anxious to see the world, starting with Philadelphia, so that's what they named me."

"Interesting," he said.

"But I accidentally named my daughter after a car," I admitted. "You're only the second human being on the planet that knows this."

"So, let me guess," he said, leaning on the railing but not letting go of my hand as he turned to face me, proving he was holding my hand on purpose and not just because he forgot he was doing it! "You named your daughter Mercedes?"

"No," I said. "Although, that would've been a better name."

"You didn't name her Ford, did you?" he asked. "Or Volkswagen?"

"No," I laughed, surprising myself. "Jetta. I thought I was filling out the parking application."

"It's a pretty name," he said.

He turned to face the railing again, and we were silent as we stood there. I flipped my hand over and held his. He squeezed my hand, and I felt something that was beyond anything I'd had set out to do on my Never-Got-To-Do list. This was something I not only never got to do, but never thought *I would ever get to do*. And it had nothing to do with his celebrity status. It had to do with me being willing to feel what I was feeling as we stood holding hands and watching the stars. The waves slapped against the side of the boat and the music from below filled the air and let the night pass so that we wouldn't have to sleep.

Chapter 23: The Guest and the Grave

"I can't thank you enough," Brake said after the three of us stepped out of the airport and watched Davenport Pets Services load up Uncle Oscar and take him to the pet morgue to await his burial. We followed in a taxi and Brake signed all the necessary papers and paid.

We still had no contacts wanting to sell their graves to Brake. "It might just take a few days," I said. "Just be patient." As soon as we arrived at our building, I grabbed a paper from the lobby. "We might have to issue another release," I said. "You know, to build momentum."

When I opened the door to the apartment, it looked smaller and duller than I'd remembered it. I hurried across the open concept apartment and pulled open the heavy drapes. Sunlight streamed in and there was a layer of dust everywhere. I'd somehow become accustomed to a maid doing all the cleaning for me on the cruise, so the thought of dusting and cleaning everything was not in the least appealing.

It was then that I noticed our Never-Got-To-Do board stuck to the wall. I hurriedly ripped it off the wall, realizing how embarrassing it would be if Brake saw *date a celebrity* written near the top of the list. I hurried into the bedroom with it and shoved it into the closet.

"I have so much cleaning to do!" I said, acting like that freakish act of ripping things off the wall and throwing them into the closet was my normal cleaning routine.

"Why don't I just get a hotel room?" he said. "Honestly, you guys don't have to put me up."

"No, no, that's perfectly fine," I insisted, afraid that if I let him out of my sight, I might never see him again. I was afraid that I might wake up and find out that this had all been some fantastic dream. The logic of *the* Brake Caldwell visiting *me* was too absurd to even process. I didn't want to leave one ounce of room for reality to sink in. I wasn't letting him get away that easily.

"I have an idea," Frankie said. "Why don't you get a cab and go out and buy a bed, while Del and I clean out the craft room?"

"I can help you clean it out," he said. "No reason why you two should do all the work."

We had to go out for lunch because I'd left no food in the apartment to spoil during our vacation. I'd briefly forgotten that Brake wasn't just an ordinary person until we walked into the diner on the corner. We hadn't even ordered before the cook came around and got Brake to take his picture with her. Then several women came over and politely asked for his autograph. He smiled and looked happy that he still had some fans.

I, on the other hand, was jealous and getting more irritated by the minute that these women actually thought it was okay to interrupt someone else's meal! *Imagine!*

"Oh, we used to do that too," Frankie nudged me and whispered in my ear. I felt my face turn red over the fact that my jealousy was that obvious.

Then we went shopping for a bed for him. The looks he got in the department store were undeniable recognition.

In the bedding section, I overheard whispers on the other side of the aisle. "I told you he was really coming here!" One woman was whispering to another. "I read it in the paper!"

I quickly steered Brake over to the other end of the store, not wanting our shopping trip interrupted by autograph-seekers, all while thinking it might've been a mistake to have put out a news release about his visit.

It was midnight when we'd finally achieved the feat of moving every bit of craft and sewing supplies out of the small bedroom, and Brake had his bed set up. He also bought a dresser, so he was able to unpack, which I took as a positive sign that he intended to stay awhile.

"The apartment is a disaster," I said to Frankie while we lay there in the middle of the night debating if Brake was asleep or not. I was tempted to go peek at him, but I didn't want him to think I was reviving my stalker habits, so I didn't.

"How long do you think he'll stay?" Frankie asked.

"I have no idea," I said. "I mean, technically, he *could* move in with us. We do have that spare room, and it would help us with the rent."

"But he's got money, he could afford to live in a much nicer place," she pointed out, and I knew she was right. Right now, he was staying with us because he was alone. Once he'd grieved for Uncle Oscar, he might just leave.

"I suppose," I said. "And if he doesn't just leave after the funeral, if he decides to stay in Davenport, he'll probably buy a house or something."

"Well, I think he likes you," Frankie said.

"What?" I exclaimed. As much as I wanted that to be true, I found it hard to believe. "He's just feeling alone over his dog," I said. "Once some time passes, he'll get back to his real life."

"I've seen the way he looks at you, Del," she said,

and then, in a mocking tone, "Oh, Philadelphia! You're ama-a-a-a-zing!"

"Oh, stop it," I said. "Do you think? Do you think he *really* does like me?"

"If you haven't noticed by now, you need to get your eyes checked!" She rolled over. "We need to get some sleep." She seemed to instantly fall asleep, while I lay there and pondered the future.

I was the last to get up in the morning and Frankie was sitting at the table with Brake having coffee. "We need to get groceries," she said. "I'll run out and get them. Tommy's picking me up, and he'll take me shopping."

I figured she was trying to give Brake and me some space.

"Oh, I got some emails," she said as I sat down with my coffee.

"Really? From Mrs. Ross?" I asked anxiously.

"No," she said. "So, I haven't answered any of them yet. But it turns out an awful lot of people have graves to sell."

"More likely, the entire city is buying graves so that they can be the one to say they did a favor for Brake Caldwell," I said with amusement.

Brake laughed. "I can't believe I have the power to make an entire city buy up all the graves."

"Don't sell yourself short," I said with a laugh. "You're not over the hill yet."

"I feel like I'm over the hill that's on *top* of the hill," he said. "Honestly, I don't know how I'd handle this if I didn't have you two."

"I'm feeling more alive than I've ever felt," Frankie said. "That cruise did me wonders!"

I watched Brake's face fall at the mention of the cruise, and that told me it would be a very long time before he would be getting on another ship. Perhaps his stay *would* be permanent. After all, Davenport was as good a city as anywhere to call home.

"Well, I better be getting ready," Frankie said awkwardly. "Tommy will be here shortly."

She disappeared into the bedroom and closed the door.

Brake drank his coffee.

"Would you like more?" I asked, but he shook his head.

"I don't know what to do with myself," he said, staring into his empty cup. "I guess I didn't think very far ahead."

"Brake! You have a bestselling book! You have friends! You can do anything you put your mind to!" I insisted. "The world is your oyster!"

"Thanks, Del," he said with a half-grin that conveyed sadness more than anything else. "Where to from here, though?"

"Well, first we get a grave!" I said.

"Well, that's usually not the first step in planning the rest of your life," he said. "But in this case, I agree, so let's get a grave!"

"Guys!" Frankie came running out of the bedroom waving her phone. "I got an email from her! It's her! Look, Mrs. Ross!"

"Read it!" I urged as Frankie sat back down at the table.

So, she did:

"Dear Brake Caldwell Team,
Allow me to introduce myself and extend warm greetings on behalf of the City of Davenport. I am Petunia Ross, head of the Davenport Literacy Council, owner

of the Davenport Ross Museum, and influential presence in this community. It would be my great pleasure to offer you, free of charge, the most beautiful cemetery spot that overlooks Davenport Bay. My offer comes with a luxury casket and marble headstone.

We would be very pleased if you would also make an appearance at the Davenport Ross Museum at your convenience, where we would be thrilled to name a wing in your honor. Please have your team contact my associates at the below email addresses to arrange a time and to finalize the paperwork for the cemetery plot.

Warmest regards,
Petunia P. Ross"

"Hootin' banana crackers!" I said. "We did it! I *told* you we could do it!"

"Del, I underestimated you!" Brake said.

"I guess that makes *me* your team," Frankie said to Brake. "I guess I will contact her *associates.*"

So, Frankie took care of the arrangements for the plot, and I helped Brake write something beautiful for the headstone, and we sent it off to Dunn Final Arrangements to have the inscription carved, and to arrange a time for the funeral.

I ended up having to call them because they insisted that they send someone to pick up the body from the morgue.

"I'm sorry," I said to Mr. Dunn. "You have to understand that this is a very high-profile funeral, being a celebrity funeral and all. The utmost privacy is required. We will send our *own* car to pick up the casket from *you* and deliver it to the morgue. Because of Mr. Caldwell's celebrity status, we cannot allow the location of his uncle to be leaked. I'm sure you understand."

"Yes, yes, of course," the man agreed readily, much more congenial on the phone than in an email.

When I hung up, I looked at Brake. "Now we need to figure out how to get our own hearse."

"Only *you* could solve a problem like needing to find your own hearse," he said with a shake of his head. "You know, I might just stick around you forever for the sheer entertainment value."

I would definitely be okay with that!

Chapter 24: The Solution

The following day, we were still trying to find a vehicle.

"We could rent a box truck," I said.

"Isn't that overkill?" Frankie asked with a raised eyebrow. "A van would probably do it. Do you think a casket could fit in a van?"

"I don't know!" I said. "How would *I* know?"

So, we did an online search for length and size of caskets.

"But how much space is in a van?" I asked.

"I don't know," she said.

"I don't either," said Brake. "I don't even drive."

"What? Don't you have your license?" I asked in surprise.

"No, I never needed it," he said.

"Oh, right, you always took limos," I said. "I can't believe I forgot who I was talking to."

He gave me a sideways look. "No, sometimes I took a cab!"

I didn't believe him, but it didn't matter. "Okay, well, we need to get this over and done with," I said.

"I'm all for that!" Brake agreed.

"I can call Tommy," Frankie offered. "He has a van."

"Do you know if is big enough to hold a casket?"

"He can take out the seats," she said.

"Okay, call him!" I urged.

She dialed and put him on speaker phone so Brake and I could keep abreast of the developments. "Hey, Tommy, do you still have the back seats out of the van?"

I raised an eyebrow at her.

"No, Mom," he said. "Why? Listen, I don't have any more room in my garage. I'm sorry but I can't take anymore of Dad's stuff. You'll have to donate them like I told you yesterday."

"No, I don't need you to store anymore stuff," she said. "I just need to borrow your van this afternoon if you're not using it?"

"Mom, you can't even drive!" he said.

"I know, but Del can," she said.

"No, Del can't drive my van," he said. "My insurance doesn't cover occasional drivers."

I could see this was not going to work.

"Well, could you drive us then to pick up something?" she asked. Brake and I both shook our heads vigorously

"That's okay!" I said. "We'll figure something else out." I made signs for her to hang up. The fewer people that knew that Uncle Oscar wasn't a dog, the better. I waved my hands and shook my head, mouthing the words *don't say anything!*

"Okay, well, how much would the van hold if you left two of the back seats in?" she asked.

"I don't know, Mom," he said. "What are you moving?"

I stood up and frantically waved my arms around until Frankie finally ended the call.

"What is *wrong* with you?" she asked.

"I have another idea," I said and ran and grabbed my laptop. "We'll just rent a hearse."

But it wasn't that easy to find a hearse rental.

"Okay, look, I found a hearse for sale," I said. "It looks like it retired twenty years ago."

"Look, there's a chunk of paint peeled off," Frankie said.

"We could paint it," I said.

"It's turning into a major expense now," Frankie said.

I looked at Brake. I'd just assumed he would pay since it was, after all, his dog.

"Hey, I'm staying out of this one," he said. "I have no ideas to help solve this problem. Sorry, girls, but I'm gonna be useless over here."

"Okay, I need a minute to think!" I said and got up and paced around the apartment. Finally, I was struck by a brilliant idea! "Okay, I have a solution!"

"This oughta be good," Frankie said.

"I'm all ears," Brake said. "Spill it."

"Okay, we only need to keep it a secret in *this* town that Uncle Oscar is coming from the vet. "We could hire a hearse from another town!"

"Yeah, but that would still get out," Frankie said. "You know it would get out."

"Okay, I have a better idea," I said. "We get Dunn's Final Arrangements to drop off the casket *here* today, and then tomorrow, we have Uncle Oscar delivered *here* and schedule it so that the hearse shows up to pick up the closed casket as soon as we get Uncle Oscar into it, and then have the funeral right away. How does that sound?"

"So, you're willing to sleep with a casket in your living room all night?" Brake asked doubtfully. "It seems kind of morbid."

"Or," Frankie said. "We could put it in the storage room!"

"There isn't enough room in there, Frankie," I said.

Her boxes filled it to the ceiling.

"There is *now!*" She said. "Yesterday when I went to get groceries, I got Tommy to take all of Edgar's boxes to his place so I could clean out the storage room to make space for all of our craft stuff."

"What?" I asked in shock. Had she really healed that much without me noticing?

"Well, I haven't been down there in ages, and since I moved in, neither one of us has even touched the craft stuff," she said. "I figured we could put it down there, at least for now, so that it isn't so cluttered up here and feels more like home."

"You did this yesterday?" I asked in shock, still trying to wrap my head around why, when, and how she did it.

"That's why I asked Tommy if he still had the seats out of the van," she said. "He took them out yesterday to move all those boxes before he took me shopping."

"Oh, wow," I said, staring at my friend. "I'm so proud of you, Frankie!"

"It was time," she said. "I feel like I'm living again."

I looked at Brake and our eyes met. I could tell he was trusting me to help him the way I'd helped Frankie, and she was living proof that things could get better.

So, we called Dunn Final Arrangements and had them drop off the casket, agreeing to pick it up the following day at 2:30 p.m. I called the Pet Services and arranged for them to drop off Uncle Oscar at 2:00 p.m. the following day.

When the hearse arrived, we got a lot of stares from other tenants coming and going from the building. But, with heads raised high, we wheeled the casket into the elevator and took it down to the storage room. The following day, Uncle Oscar was dropped off in the parking garage and we carried the box into the storage room. By the time we opened the box, Brake was in tears.

Uncle Oscar looked the same, just ice cold and still. I helped him lift the dog into the casket and get him situated.

"Wait!" Frankie said. "Don't close it yet! I'll be right back."

She ran out of the room. I had no idea where she was going, but I didn't ask. I just sat silently and watched Brake run his fingers over his beloved pet's forehead. When he broke down in tears, I passed him the remnants of a box of tissues that Frankie had left there from her days down here crying. He tried to choke back his tears but failed.

"I'll give you a minute," I said, going out and guarding the door while I waited for Frankie to come back. I had no idea what to say to Brake. I knew that if I were in his shoes, though, I would want to have time to cry in private over the one I'd lost.

Finally, Frankie returned carrying Edgar's pajamas and a suit. "I had kept the suit in the closet," she said. "But I hadn't counted on needing it."

I tapped on the door, and we went in. "I brought these for him to wear," Frankie said. Brake looked surprised but wiped his face with a tissue. He looked so sad as he reached for the clothes, and I knew that Frankie had done the right thing.

"Thank you so much," he said.

Brake was too upset to decide whether it made sense or not, and I was too surprised to decide if it made sense or not, but somehow to Frankie, it made sense to wrap the dog in blue plaid pajamas and a suit jacket, with the pants folded neatly at his feet. "In case they ask why we had to do it this way," she said. "We can say we had to put him in his best suit. And we won't be lying."

I checked the time on Brake's watch. "The hearse will be here in a few minutes." I said. The three of us kneeled beside the casket and cried. I put my arm around Brake so that he'd know I was there for him for as long as he wanted me to be. I put my other arm around Frankie because I knew that somehow this was her way of burying Edgar.

The three of us sat there and waited for the hearse. I never thought that at 62, I would be sitting in a parking garage storage room on my knees with a movie star and my best friend from school, sobbing over a canine in casket.

Chapter 25: The Funeral

It had been such a whirlwind in the past few days, that I hadn't even had chance to talk to Jetta other than a quick text to let her know I was home. Because hearses drive reverently slowly, I called Jetta during the drive through the city.

"Hey, Mom, how was your trip?" she asked brightly.

"Great, listen, do you want to go to a funeral?" I asked in a rush.

"Excuse me? What?" she asked.

"Sorry, I'm short on time," I said. "Long story short, I got the grave back from Mrs. Ross like I promised you I would, but we have to fill it before she changes her mind. We are on the way right now to have a funeral there. Do you want to attend?"

"Um, okay, Mom, I'm in the middle of baking," she said. *"Whose* funeral?"

"Okay, have you heard of Brake Caldwell?" I asked. "Have you even been reading the paper?"

"Not really," she said. "I've been super busy, Mom. Look, when is the funeral and I'll try to schedule it."

"It will be held in about fifteen minutes," I said. "If you don't want to miss it, you better come now!"

"Okay, hang on," she said. "Okay, David will babysit the kids, and I'll be right there."

We drove in silence to the graveyard.

"It's good it's short notice," I said. "Or probably the

entire city would be here."

We followed the hearse through the gates of the cemetery and through the winding gravel road that led up the hill to the prime location in the center.

"You *can* see the ocean from here," Brake noted in surprise. "I'm glad Uncle Oscar has a good spot."

"Me too," I said, patting his hand as I pulled over to the edge of the road behind the hearse. It was at that moment that I realized we didn't have any pallbearers. "Rats!" I called Jetta back. "Can you bring David?" I asked. "I forgot we need pallbearers."

"But who will sit the kids?" she asked.

"You must have a sitter!" I said. Organized Jetta didn't have a sitter on call?

"Give me a few minutes," she said. "Don't start without us then!"

"I'll call Tommy," Frankie offered, so she stepped away a little and called her son.

"Okay, that makes three of us," Brake said. "We need three more."

"Well, Frankie and I will!" I said. I glanced at Frankie, and she nodded as she hung up.

"Tommy's on his way," she said. "Yes, Del and I can help carry it."

"Okay, we need one more," Brake said.

Somehow the word had gotten out, and a string of cars turned into the cemetery driveway. "Oh dear," I said. "I hadn't expected to get such a turnout! Remember, not a *word* of who Uncle Oscar *is!*"

When I saw Mrs. Ross and Mayor John R. Turner step out of the first car, I had an idea. *Could I? It was only fitting!*

"Hang on, you guys," I said to Brake and Frankie. "I have a solution!"

I hurried over to Mrs. Ross. "Hello," I said. "You must be Mrs. Ross. I'm one of Mr. Caldwell's representatives."

"Hello," she said while her eyes scanned the gathering crowd for Brake. "I'm anxious to meet him."

"He asks that you respect his privacy at this difficult time," I said.

"Oh, of course!" she said. "Oh, here come the reporters!"

"Mrs. Ross," I said, before she hurried away to talk to the reporters. "I'm wondering if you could help us find a sixth pallbearer for Brake's dear Uncle Oscar?"

"Of course!" She said, obviously pleased that I trusted her to solve a problem for such a high-profile celebrity. "Just leave it with me!"

I headed back to Brake and Frankie.

"What was that all about?" Frankie asked.

"Mrs. Ross is going to get us the mayor to be a pallbearer," I said.

"She said that?" Frankie asked in shock.

"Nope," I said, watching Mrs. Ross scurry through the crowd. "But she *will!*"

"How do you know that?" Brake asked.

"Because the higher profile person she gets to do this favor for a celebrity, the higher profile *she* will have as the person that arranged it," I said. "She is all about power and attention. Just watch."

Tommy arrived. "Mom!" he said, as he hopped out of his van and raced to Frankie. "What happened?"

While she was introducing him to Brake and explaining who died, David sond Jetta showed up.

With reserved dignity, wearing appropriate funeral black, they walked over to us. "Who died?" Jetta whispered to me.

"Uncle Oscar," I explained.

"Who is Uncle Oscar?" he asked.

"Brake's beloved uncle," I said. "Jetta, this is Brake Caldwell. Brake, this is my daughter, Jetta, and her husband, David." Brake shook their hands.

"Thank you for coming," he said.

"Hello," Mrs. Ross said loudly as she interrupted our family gathering. "I would like to present to you Mayor Jonathan R. Turner," she said and pushed her way directly to Brake. "Well, how lovely to meet you, Brake Caldwell! This is our mayor, Mayor Jonathan R. Turner, and he is happy to act as pallbearer for your uncle."

"Thank you so much," Brake said, shaking the mayor's hand.

"My condolences," the mayor said, and then proceeded to shake all of our hands, offering condolences to all while Tommy, David and the hearse driver pulled the casket out onto its gurney.

"Are we ready?" Mrs. Ross asked loudly as if she were directing a grade school theatrical performance. "The mayor should go first, of course, on this side," she said pointing to the front left of the casket. "And Mr. Caldwell, of course you should be first on that side. Then, you, here," she pointed to me and to the middle handle on the casket.

"No!" Brake said loudly. "I want her up front, with me."

"Well, the casket will be too heavy in the front," Mrs. Ross said. "It needs to be balanced out so that the men are bearing the brunt of the weight at the front and the back."

Judging from the long line of Ross graves, it was clear she had become an expert in pallbearing choreography.

"Then, find another man," he said. "Del, I'd like you to walk beside me, if you're okay with that."

"Absolutely!" I said and hurried over to his side. He reached out and took my hand. I was pleased with the way he didn't let Mrs. Ross walk all over him.

"Frankie, are you okay there?" Brake asked her. "If you want, you can walk beside Del, and we can get a man to carry it."

"No, I *need* to do this," she said with firm determination, and I knew that although she'd bonded with Brake's pet, this was more than just about Uncle Oscar. This was also about Edgar. And about moving forward and burying the past. I understood that this was something she felt she *had* to do, and I respected that.

Mrs. Ross went rummaging through the crowd of fans for another strong man. She soon returned with a beefy man about half our age. It wasn't until he was right in front of me that I recognized the big beefy man to be Richard! *My Mailman!* "Everyone, this is Mr. Parker," she announced. "Mr. Parker, this is Brake Caldwell." She didn't bother introducing him to the rest of us. "Mr. Parker, you'll be right here, okay?" She walked away before he even acknowledged that it was indeed okay. Richard smiled at me and Frankie.

"My condolences on your loss," he said to us.

"Thank you so much, Richard," I said.

"Oh, good heavens!" Mrs. Ross said, rushing over to us. "Where's your minister!"

"It was just supposed to be a private burial," Brake said. "We don't have a minister."

"One minute," she said, and I was beginning to resent that she was so adept at problem solving. Soon she returned with a man in a suit. "This is Derek," she introduced him. "He's a Baptist minister, and he says he's happy to do the committal service."

When everyone was ready, under Mrs. Ross's direction, I walked beside Brake, clutching his hand, and his best friend got the funeral he was worthy of.

When the casket was set on the lowering straps, we all stepped back on the side of the grave opposite the still-growing crowd.

Unprepared for the sudden funeral, the minister didn't have a bible on him. He recited a few scriptures and then said a prayer for the grieving family, and while Brake, Frankie and I cried for the end of Uncle Oscar's life, the minister tried to offer words of comfort. "I like to believe that our Creator has a specific day, hour, and second for us to come into this world, and he also has a specific day, hour, and second for us to return to Him," he said gently. "We never really lose those we love; we just carry all the love they gave us in our hearts for the rest of our lives, and they live on through us."

When he'd finished speaking, he asked if anyone would like to say a few words. Brake stepped forward. "Uncle Oscar was my best friend," he said, his words broken by tears. "He was always there when I needed him. He looked after me when my father passed away, and he stayed with me all these years."

I hoped that Brake wouldn't forget that all these people were assuming Uncle Oscar was a *man* and let something slip that would clarify that he was a dog.

"I will never forget you, Uncle Oscar," Brake said and kissed his fingers and touched the casket. "Happy trails."

He stepped back and clutched my hand, I squeezed back and handed him a tissue. To my surprise, Frankie stepped forward.

"I didn't get to spend as much time with Uncle Oscar as Brake did," she said. "But Uncle Oscar helped me start to heal from my own grief over my husband's death.

Goodbye, Uncle Oscar." She kissed her fingers and touched his casket and stepped back.

Now I felt awkward. I didn't have anything to say. I hadn't been close to the dog. But I felt like I had to say *something*. I took a step forward with a blank mind and swallowed hard.

"I didn't know Uncle Oscar very well at all," I admitted, reminding myself not to give too much away. "But I will never forget the first time I met him. I thought he might be a ghost."

I looked back at Frankie who smiled, and Brake gave me a quizzical look.

"But what I do know is that he has left a huge hole in the hearts of the people I care about. Thank you, Uncle Oscar, for being so loving." I kissed my fingers and touched the casket, copying Brake and Frankie, and stepped back. Brake grabbed my hand and squeezed.

Just as the casket was about to be lowered, Mrs. Ross stepped forward. *Of course, she would have something to say!*

"It was many years ago that I met Oscar .... Caldwell," she lied. "And when I tell you that there was no one sweeter, you can believe it! He was the kindest friend anyone could hope for. We were engaged once, but alas, he chose to go to sea! Goodbye, my beloved!" She held her fingers to her lips and then reached out and touched the casket in a huge gesture of mourning, then she dabbed at the corners of her eyes with a handkerchief, looking theatrically heartbroken.

"Oh brother!" I mumbled, and Frankie jabbed me in the side with her elbow.

The crowd dispersed as the casket was lowered into the ground. Frankie and Brake sobbed on either side of me, but I choked back tears. I hated to cry in front of others. Especially when Mrs. Ross remained at the graveside to make it look like she had a connection to Uncle Oscar.

"We have to leave," I whispered to Brake. "They won't cover it until we do."

"I can't," he said. "I can't just leave him like this. I have to stay until it's done."

We stepped aside a little as the grave workers filled in the soil. Brake sobbed into my hair as he wrapped his arms around me, and Frankie sobbed beside us, processing her own grief at last.

"We are having a gathering at the town hall," Mrs. Ross said with feigned sorrow. "There will be refreshments."

"No thank you," Brake said in a raspy voice. "We just want privacy please."

Mrs. Ross looked offended but at least she left.

"Are you ready to go?" I asked him. It was then that I noticed we were standing almost on Fred's grave. I felt a pang of guilt for never having come to his grave.

Jetta came over to me and put her arms around me. "I love you, Mom," she said.

"I love you, too, sweetie," I said, patting her arm. "I'll explain everything later. Thank you so much for coming."

"Of course," she said. "That's what family's for!"

And then Brake and me, and Frankie, and Tommy, and Jetta and David all walked back to our vehicles.

"I'll give you a ride home, Mom," Tommy said to Frankie. She nodded at me, and I nodded back. I knew she was giving me time to be alone with Brake, and I appreciated it.

"Call me," Jetta said as she headed for her car with David. I promised I would. "You have to tell me how you got that grave back."

I nodded. "I just have one more thing to do," I said and walked back over to Fred's grave.

I stared at his headstone. His name and birthdate and death date were all that was written there. No flowery words of love or how he was missed, like on Uncle Oscar's headstone. I realized that despite all Fred's flaws and selfishness, he was truly gone, and he had just been a human after all. Humans are never meant to be perfect. Just because he wasn't a good husband, he still had value as a human being.

"I forgive you," I whispered and was surprised that the weight I'd carried on my heart unknowingly was lifted.

I turned and walked back to Brake, who was leaning against the car, giving me space.

"Are you okay?" he asked gently, wrapping his arm around my shoulders when I reached him.

"I am now," I said, and we got into the car, leaving the past where it belonged.

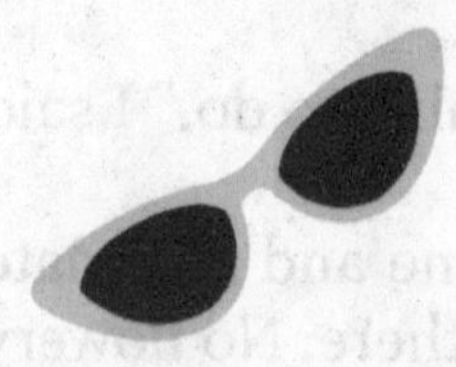

Chapter 26: Listless

The following morning, Brake slept in, and Frankie was just leaving to spend the morning with her grandkids when Jetta showed up.

"Mom! I just googled your friend, and did you know he used to be famous?" Jetta asked as soon as she stepped through the door. She quickly looked around with a red face before breathing a sigh of relief, seeing that I was alone. "Mom! Did you know?"

"Have a seat, Jetta," I offered and poured her some coffee, although, judging by her high-pitched excitement, she'd already had a cup or two. "Well, let's just say I had an inkling, considering my bedroom walls were plastered with his posters when I was a teenager."

She looked at me like I'd somehow wronged her by not divulging my secret fangirl past. "Of course I knew that!" I said.

"Okay, spill the beans," she said, as I placed her cup in front of her and sat down across from her with my own. "I want to know everything! *How on earth* did you manage to get the grave plot back from Mrs. Ross?"

I shoved the morning paper across the table to her. "Well, it seems she'd do anything to get in the paper," I said. She looked at the front-page headline that read *Highly Coveted Plot Goes to Old Flame of Prominent Local*.

Jetta read it and looked at the photo of Mrs. Ross standing between the mayor and Brake. "Old flame?" she asked. "She had an affair with Brake Caldwell's uncle?"

"No," I said, shaking my head and laughing.

"Well, I wouldn't be too sure," Jetta said. "You *do* know what she's like."

"I know," I said. "But I can guarantee she didn't."

"Why?" Jetta eyed me suspiciously. "Was he not into women?"

"Pretty sure he wasn't," I said. "Besides, he was a dog."

I waited for her laugh, but instead she scowled. "Mom, it isn't nice to talk ill of the dead," she scolded.

"I'm not," I said slowly, realizing she thought I meant Uncle Oscar was some sort of scoundrel. "Uncle Oscar was a wonderful, caring companion, Jetta. But he was *literally* a dog. He was Brake's pet. He had no place to bury him, so I figured what better way to get that grave back from her—like I promised you I would—than to capitalize on her need to be the center of everyone's attention."

"So, she gave up her spot next to Dad for a *dog?*" Jetta asked with disbelief written all over her face. "And why would she pretend she dated him?"

"Well, first, she not only claims to have dated him," I pointed down to the third paragraph on the page. "Apparently, she was also engaged to him in college. And also, she has no idea that Uncle Oscar is a dog."

"Mom!" Jetta exclaimed, and I didn't know if she was appalled that I was willing to con someone out of a grave, or if she was pleased that at least Mrs. Ross wouldn't be parked next to her father for eternity. "That's genius!"

"Well, I promised you I'd get it back," I reminded her. "And I always keep my promises."

"But," Jetta looked at me with mixture of awe and adoration. "You got the *mayor* to be a pallbearer for a *dog!* Is there anything you *can't* do?"

"Jetta, I thought you knew me by now," I said with a laugh. "I don't believe that there's anything *anyone* can't do!"

"So," she said when she'd sipped enough coffee to process everything she'd witnessed. "How did you meet Brake Caldwell?"

"On the cruise," I said.

"So, are you guys . . .*a thing?*" she asked.

"We're *something,*" I said. "Right now, he's grieving, and I'm being his friend. We'll see what happens."

"I'm not used to seeing you so reserved," she said.

"Maybe I'm growing up a little," I said with a laugh.

"I hope not," she said. "Despite your tendency to bring chaos into my life, I like you the way you are."

We laughed. "Oh, hey, since you're here, why don't you help me carry all this craft stuff down to the storage room?"

"Sure," she agreed, finishing her coffee. "Let's go! I have some errands to run, so let's get this done."

She seemed different, but I couldn't put my finger on the difference. It was a good difference for sure. "Jetta," I asked as we stepped into the elevator. "Did you actually *miss* me while I was gone?"

"Yes," she admitted. "It was the first time you weren't just around the corner, and I could call you if I needed you."

"*Did* you need me?" I asked. Instant remorse for not being there for my daughter in any time of need raced through my brain.

"I *always* need you," she said. "But, no, everything is fine."

The way she said it was fine made me worry. "Just *fine* and not *great?*" I asked. She had a perfect home, career, and family, with another child on the way. *What could possibly be missing?*

"It's fine" she said with a shake of her head as we stepped out of the elevator into the garage.

"Why do you not sound like it's fine?" I asked.

"Oh, really, Mom, it's nothing," she insisted, setting the boxes down. "David and I just had our first fight, that's all."

"*What?*" I shrieked.

"I know, shocking right?" she asked. "What would we possibly have to fight about?"

"No, I mean, you've been married for *eight years,* and you guys just had your *first* fight?" I was aware that my jaw was hanging open.

"Yeah," she said in the same tone she might've used if I'd just asked her if her house had a roof. "So?"

"Let me tell you, Jetta," I said, wrapping my arms around her. "Are you happy?"

"Of course!" she exclaimed like I'd insulted her.

"Then you're doing everything right!" I said. "And I'm so proud of you."

We left the storage room with a renewed sense of familial strength. I loved that she still needed me, if only just to be right around the corner, and she knew how proud I was of her.

"I have to get to the post office," she said. "But why don't you come with me, and then we can go to lunch like we used to before Nathan was born?"

"Okay," I agreed and off we went.

It was hours later when she dropped me off at the front of the building. It was then that I'd realized I hadn't even grabbed my purse or cell phone when we'd left, so I didn't have my keys. I buzzed the apartment hoping that Brake hadn't decided to go out for a walk or something.

"Hello?" It was Frankie.

"It's me!" I yelled at the intercom.

She buzzed the door open, and I headed up.

As soon as I opened the door, the first thing I saw was the big posterboard with the Never-Got-To-Do list standing on the table where Brake and Frankie were sitting having coffee.

"What are you guys doing?" I asked as casually as possible. And it wasn't really possible to sound casual with my eyes popping out of my head.

"Oh," Frankie said and pointed to the list. "Somehow this got accidentally thrown in the closet. I'm just explaining it to Brake. I think *he* should make a Never-Got-To-Do List too."

I swallowed hard as I noticed that Frankie had checked off *Date a Celebrity*. "Oh?" was all I could squeak out.

Brake eyed me with a teasing smile. "I take it *I'm* the celebrity you wanted to date," he said with raised eyebrows.

"To be honest, I had no idea I would meet you," I said coolly.

Frankie gave me a questioning stare.

"Is that a fact?" he asked.

My heart raced, and I felt my face burning up. I had no idea what Frankie had already told him, so I wasn't sure what to say. *Maybe I could gloss over it, and he might forget whatever they'd discussed while I was gone.*

"Let's see," I said. "How many more do we have to do? Oh, you know what? The cruise was really the most important thing *I* wanted to do, and we've done most of them anyway, so let's just throw this away."

I grabbed the posterboard, as big and awkward as it was, and turned toward the bedroom. "I'm just going to go have a quick shower," I said. "It's been a long morning."

I hurried into the bedroom with a beet-red face, dragging the awkward sized list through the door. I locked the door and realized I was holding my breath. I let it out in one long forced exhale.

I was so embarrassed. Now how do I face him? He probably just thinks he's some checkmark on a list. Frankie just blew all the legitimate progress I'd made! Why, why, why did she have to show him the list?

I paced the bedroom floor. *Now what would I do?* I couldn't face Brake again. I was too humiliated now that he knew I'd purposely set out to date a celebrity. It sure didn't help that I'd already confessed to stalking him. I couldn't face him again. The stuff on the list seemed so silly now.

- Be in a movie
- date a celebrity
- ride in a limo
- walk the red carpet
- go on a cruise
- sign autographs
- publish a book
- go on vacation in Hawaii
- Stay in a luxury hotel

These were all things he'd done a million times, and I probably looked like a silly child for even *wanting* to do any of this stuff.

I dug through my nightstand drawer for a pen and crossed off everything I'd done, as well as everything I *hadn't* done. I had no desire now to pursue any of these things. *Publish a book! As if anyone would even want to read something I wrote!* That would have to remain on a Never-Gonna-Do List! Even if it was Frankie's list too, she could make her *own* list and find a way to follow her *own* dreams. I was tired of trying to make things better for everyone else. *How dare she show him something so personal?*

Even as I fumed over Frankie's insensitivity, I was aware that I was still emotional over the funeral. Sure, it was for a dog that wasn't even mine, but I'd felt so many emotions watching Brake cry, watching Frankie try to get some closure on her own loss, and the way our families had rushed to our sides at a moment's notice for something they didn't even understand.

"Hey." Brake's voice mumbled its way through my door along with a brief tap. "Can I come in?"

He was the *last* person I wanted to face right now. I didn't answer. Maybe he'll go away.

"Del?" he asked. "I really think we should talk."

Of course he does! He probably wanted to tell me he was going to move into a hotel. He probably thought he saw through a flimsy attempt to keep him to myself and make him all mine.

He knocked again. "Philadelphia," he said lightly. "I know you're in there."

I steeled myself for the discussion and the pending loss. It's no big deal, I decided. I wasn't even that close to him. It's not like we were lovers or anything. Who cares what he thinks?

When I'd sufficiently worked my thoughts around to the reality of the situation, I took a deep breath and opened the door. "Yes?" I asked as calmly as if we were about to discuss what to have for dinner.

"Can we talk?" he asked. I looked around but Frankie was gone. "Frankie had to go run an errand and file some paperwork. Seems she hadn't filed the paperwork to collect her husband's spousal benefits."

"*What?*" I shrieked. "She told me it was a bureaucratic error!"

"Yeah, hers, apparently," he said with a lopsided

grin. "So, it's just you and me, so can we talk? Honestly and openly?"

"Go ahead," I said, bracing myself for what was to come.

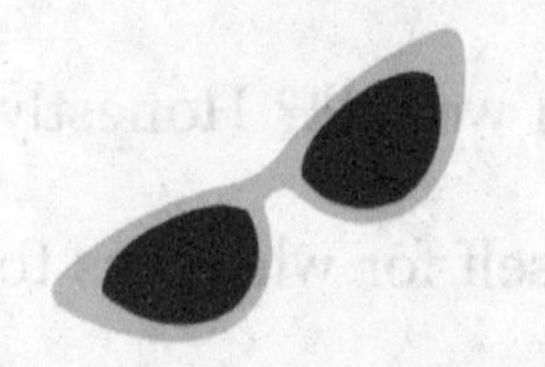

Chapter 27: Love and Lists

I made coffee to keep my hands busy and provide me with a justifiable way to not face Brake.

"Do you have some paper and a pen?" he asked as I busied myself at the counter, dragging out my coffee-stirring as long as was humanly possible.

"Yes, there's a notebook and pens in that desk drawer over there," I said. And then, as he started to stand up from the table, I was filled with panic over the thought that I could've possibly jotted some embarrassing thought that I wouldn't want him to see. "Sit back down, I'll get it," I said and rushed to the entryway, yanking out a blank piece of paper and a pen.

At least while he was writing, I had a good excuse for not looking at him. *I'm giving him privacy,* I told myself. I wiped down the counters and emptied the dish strainer and washed the few coffee cups from earlier. Still unable to face him, I grabbed the dry mop and proceeded to slowly wipe down the kitchen floor. I was heading to the closet to pull out the vacuum to clean the living room carpet when Brake caught my arm. "Please, Del, sit down?" he asked.

Better get it over with! I grabbed my coffee and sat down at the table across from him.

"You know what this is?" he held up his sheet of paper with a list on it.

"A list?" I said.

"It's *my* Never-Got-To-Do list," he said. *Now he*

was mocking me?

I got up. "You don't need to make fun of me," I said. "My list might seem silly to you, but I didn't have the luxuries of growing up in Hollywood like you did! I spent all my time raising my daughter and working hard, sometimes working two jobs at a time! I didn't have time nor money to live a rich celebrity life! So, I'm sorry if my hopes and dreams seem ridiculous to you!"

I fled to the bedroom, but before I reached the door, he caught me by the shoulder. "Philadelphia," he said gently. "Please don't judge me until you let me read *my* list. Please? I'm not making fun of you! I just want you to see what *my* never got to do's are."

"Fine," I said, reeking of embarrassment.

"Let's just sit down here on the sofa," he said, steering me by the shoulders to the living room. "I promise, if you want to run to your room when I'm done, I'll let you. If you tell me to move out, I'll go. But please, just listen first?"

"Fine," I repeated and folded my arms.

"Okay," he said, holding up the pen and the list. "Number one. I never got to live in a real apartment like a normal person," he said and checked it off. "Two, I never got to meet someone who was willing to move heaven and earth to make their friends happy." He checked it off.

"Three," he said. "I never got to have a real friend that genuinely cared about me for me." He checked it off.

"Four," he said. "I never got to go on a date with a stalker." He checked that off with a wide grin, and I remembered on the ship when I'd admitted I'd been stalking him.

"Five," he said. "I've never known *anyone* that loved with all their heart." He checked it off.

"Six," he continued. "I have never known anyone

who could always find a solution for everything, no matter what the situation was." He checked it off.

"And Seven," he said. "I never got to really fall in love."

He stared into my eyes as he slowly put a huge check mark beside that one.

I bit my lip to keep back the tears that were welling in my eyes.

"And last," he said as he set the list and pen down on the coffee table. His voice was lower, huskier now. He stared into my eyes as he moved slowly towards me. "I've never known Philadelphia Powers."

I no longer wanted to run to my room. I was ready for whatever lay ahead when Brake Caldwell lowered his lips to mine.

The End

Note from the Author

Dear Reader,

Thank you so much for taking the time to read this book. I do hope you enjoyed this adventure of Del and Frankie as much as I have! There are many more adventures for these two on the way!

If you've been a long-time reader of my books under my previous pen-name, Aspen Faraway, you will know how much I've struggled to keep up with my blog. I have found a solution, though. Open Diary! I love writing in diaries, so it is easy for me to keep up with that, as opposed to trying to keep up with a blog.

The links will be posted on my site as soon as it is up, but while I'm working on my website at

https://www.elizabethbarstone.com and all links will be available at the Haven Street Publishing website.

Yes, I'm finally giving in to years of advice that I'd refused to follow and starting a mailing list so readers can get updates when new books are released. I don't have enough interesting stuff to put in weekly, or any kind of regular newsletters, so you don't have to worry about getting tons of junk mail from me. It will only be whenever a new book comes out.

Again, thank you so much for taking the time to read this book. You have no idea how much I appreciate you!

Love,
Elizabeth Barstone

Other Books

Elizabeth Barstone
> The Time-Travel Trail Bride

Aspen Faraway
> Brothers of Atlantis
> Diary of a Teenage Mom series (11 books)
> The Wishing Field
> Diary of a Teenage Millionaire
> Delaney Page & The Secret of Everything

> Check out all of our books at Haven Street Publishing at https://www.havenstreetpublishing.com